Brimster Tales

Brimster Tales

James Miller

Illustrated by Sally Orr

Birlinn

First published in 2004 by
Birlinn Limited
West Newington House
10 Newington Road
Edinburgh EH9 1QS
www.birlinn.co.uk

ISBN 1 84158 312 X

British Library Cataloguing-in-Publication Data
A catalogue record for this book is available from the British Library

Typeset in Galliard
Layout: Mark Blackadder

Printed and bound by AIT Nørhaven A/S, Viborg

Introduction

Brimster Tales first appeared in the *John O'Groat Journal* on 4 August 2000, where it continues. I am deeply grateful to the editor, Alan Hendry, for his enthusiasm and support for the slightly daft notion of publishing a local soap opera in prose.

Anyone who looks for Brimster on a map of Caithness will be disappointed.

James Miller

August

Dougie Bayne paused as he came out from the byre and looked at the morning. The grey clouds showed signs of breaking up, promising sunshine later. In his hand the crofter carried a milking pail. Around three-quarters of a pint of milk lay in the bottom of it, and the cat rubbed against Dougie's left ankle, mewing in hope of a sip.

It was goat's milk. The goat had been Alison's idea – he raised calves for beef and allowed them to suckle the two cows he kept. The goat, christened Annabella after a long-dead aunt Alison had disliked and who, she said, had borne a distinct resemblance to the animal, had not had a kid for over a year but was still producing milk in small quantities. Enough for tea and coffee, said Alison, and good for the health, being high in unsaturated fat, but Dougie disliked the flavour in his tea and preferred to open a carton.

Annabella came out from the byre behind him and looked up at him with a wistful expression. She was a knowing animal. He was quite fond of her and kittled her ear with his hand. Maybe she was lonely, having no other goats to mix with, but she seemed to get on well with the two cows.

*   *   *

As Dougie made his way to the kitchen with the milk, two miles away, in his house in the middle of the village, Sinclair Cattach pushed aside the marmalade and the cat, reached for his writing pad and began to draft a letter to the *Groat*.

'My dear sir,' he wrote – with a stub of pencil. 'I have made a significant discovery that I feel may be of great benefit to your readers of mature years who suffer from fatigue, insomnia, tiredness and lethargy. This what I have discovered has not been published in any book I have read . . .'

His research had encompassed every likely book in the house – from Whitaker's Almanack (1938 edition) to the Bible.

'. . . but nowhere have I found mention of it. In short, I have discovered it myself. I suffered from fatigue, insomnia etc., as mentioned above, until one day I chanced to turn the bed and thereafter all my distressing symptoms disappeared. Pondering on this, I happened to notice that I had turned the bed inadvertently so as to align it in a north–south direction, whereas previously it had stood easterly–westerly. Therein lay the key.'

Cattach's excitement had mounted as the words had appeared and as he wrote 'key' the pencil could bear no more pressure and the point broke.

'Damn,' he muttered.

*   *   *

The Council dustcart reached the harbour. Pogo and Dreep got down from the cab and made their way to the wheelie bin tied to a steel post at the end of the quay. It was the first one of the day, the first of dozens they would empty in the course of their round. Pogo took a drag on his roll-up and looked about him.

'Looks like rain,' he said.

'That's richt, cheer me up some more,' growled Dreep. 'Rain is all we need on top o that grumblan walrus in the cab.'

Lang Tam, the driver, old enough to be the father of both Pogo and Dreep, was not always very good company in the morning.

Dreep detached the bin from the post and lifted the lid. Later in the day, in the village where anybody could be watching, there would be few opportunities to have a look on the off-chance of finding an object, in Dreep's opinion, too good for the dump and just right for the next car boot sale. But now he saw something that froze him to the spot.

'Hurry up,' called Pogo.

Dreep's mouth opened but no sound came from it.

'Fit is it?'

Dreep's free hand rose from his side and his finger, trembling slightly, pointed. 'Wid ye come and look at this? Tell me I'm dreaman.'

*   *   *

Dougie poured the goat's milk into a jug and placed it in the fridge to cool. He switched on the kettle. Alison came into the kitchen, still in her dressing gown.

'Ye all richt?' asked Dougie, suddenly aware that she looked very solemn.

'I think blooming or radiant is what I should be, if what they say is true,' she answered.

'Fit ye gettan at?'

'You'd better sit down, Dougie.'

'Is something wrong?'

Alison gave him a wry smile. 'No, not exactly wrong. I think I'm pregnant.'

'How?'

'What do you mean how? You're a crofter and you don't know?'

'No . . . I mean,' he looked at her for a long moment. She looked beautiful with her hair just that way. 'Alison, will ye marry me?'

*   *   *

Sinclair Cattach looked at the broken pencil in disgust and then scrabbled for a biro he knew to be lurking under the fan of papers, plates and utensils on his kitchen table. The cat growled softly at being disturbed. He apologised to him, and then found the missing pen.

'Therein lay the key,' he read the last few words he had written before the pencil point had broken, and dragged the biro across the paper. It left no mark. He held the pen in the tea for a minute and started again.

'. . . I realised that by orientating my bed in a north–south direction,' he wrote, 'I was lying at right angles to the direction of rotation of the globe. This meant that the forces of drag and friction which act on all fluids were acting with equal strength on my head and my feet, and hence on all my body fluids throughout my body. When my bed lay east–west, there was an unequal application of this force. Hence with my head to the east, my blood tended to collect at my feet, and vice versa. These tides of body fluids caused me fatigue.'

'It's so simple,' he said out loud to the cat who was at that moment more interested in dislodging the lid from the margarine tub than in the effects of gravitation on human body fluids.

'I might be able to patent a bed on gimbals that would always line up with the North Pole,' went on Cattach. 'Computerised of course.'

*   *   *

Alison stared at Dougie for a moment.

'I said – will ye marry me?' he repeated. 'I meant til ask ye at the Millennium but somehow it didna arise.'

'You were too drunk,' she said.

'Well, maybe a bittie,' he admitted. 'There's your goat's milk.'

Alison sat down at the table and swept her fingers through her hair. 'We've lived together for three years. Why ask me now?'

Dougie started to roll a fag. 'Now ye're expectan.' He shrugged. 'It seems the richt thing til do.'

'That'll have to stop.'

'What?'

'Tobacco smoke's bad for bairns.'

'Oh aye.' He put the papers into the tin and snapped the lid shut. Then he looked at her across the table. 'Well, will ye, then?'

Alison stretched her arm between the plates and gripped his fingers. 'I love you, you big dope. God knows why but I do.'

He smiled at her. 'Is that a yes?'

'Come here.'

*   *   *

'It's a boot,' said Pogo, glancing into the wheelie bin.

'It's more than a boot,' answered Dreep. 'Look at it fae my side.'

Pogo frowned and moved his position. 'What's that dark stuff?'

'I think it's blood.'

'Geez!' Pogo turned away as if he had been stung and his face whitened like a maa's.

As his companion wrapped his arms tightly around his middle and gulped air to calm the boaking in his throat, Dreep dropped the lid shut and ran to the cab of the dustcart. 'Tam!'

Lang Tam hated anything that interrupted his routine. Now instead of two hard slaps on the side of the vehicle to tell him to start moving this gowk of a binman was shouting about something.

'We need to find a phone.'

'A phone?' echoed Tam. 'Fit d'ye want a phone for?'

'We should have a mobile.'

'This bliddy cert is fit should be mobile, no a phone. Fit's keepan ee?'

Dreep's long face was creased in concern, staring up at the driver. 'It's a boot. But it's got a feet in it.'

This information began to penetrate Tam's mind – too slowly for Dreep.

'It's a feet. Somebody's left their feet in their boot and it's in the bin. It looks like a size nine.'

No response from Tam.

'I think we've got til tell some chiel,' went on Dreep.

At last Tam engaged the clutch and drove up the road from the harbour, Dreep hanging on to the door and Pogo hirpling after them. There was a phone box in the village but Dreep found it was out of order, and that left the shop. He rushed in, sending the bell above the door into a paroxysm of dinging and startling Jean behind the counter.

'Dial 999,' shouted Dreep.

'Has there been an accident?'

Dreep paused. 'Sort o,' he said.

'Well,' demanded Jean. 'Is it fire, police or ambulance ye want?

I'm no makan a fool o myself. It's no a joke, is it?'

'It's a boot wi a feet in it,' said Dreep. 'Eh . . . I think it better be police. It's too late – kinda – for an ambulance.'

Jean glowered at the young man, all legs and arms and face, and picked up the phone with great deliberation. 'Keep your hands off that papers,' she said. 'Ye're covered in muck and I can smell grease and fishguts off ye.'

'It's an emergency.'

'It better be,' she warned, and proceeded to punch the 9 button three times.

*　　*　　*

The bobbies came and went. They took statements from Pogo, Dreep and Lang Tam, who was a little uncooperative as he hated having his routine disturbed. By the time the bobbies had retrieved the boot containing the foot from the bin and had driven off with it in a plastic bag, Tam was fit for tying. 'Come on,' he shouted. 'We've got a round til do.'

But Pogo was still deep in slow thought: 'What I want til ken is how it got ere. It didna walk.'

'It micht have hopped,' suggested Dreep with a grin.

'D'ye think there micht be a reward?'

'Reward!' cried Tam in disgust. 'What for? D'ye think some chiel wants it back? Is he going til stick it on and say thanks a million, boys, here's a tenner for a pint til yoursels? Come on, or every wifie between here and Groats'll be complainan at her bin hasna been emptied.'

'I can just hear them,' said Pogo. '"Ye're no at your usual time".'

Tam switched on the engine and revved angrily. 'Let's go – and dinna open any more bliddy bins. It's wir job til empty them, no look in them.'

*　　*　　*

The news did not take long to spread around Brimster. After all, it wasn't every day that a human foot, by all appearances a fresh one, appeared in a wheelie bin. Bowser Clett, skipper of the *Polaris*, and Wildy Ham, skipper of the *Girl Ina*, were the two men who spent most time at the harbour where the offending bin stood, but neither of them had seen a soul or a thing. They said as much to Sinclair Cattach when he spoke to them in the Brimster Arms.

'It's a deep and mysterious mystery,' said Cattach, his eyes cast towards the crack in the ceiling tiles. 'Nearly as mysterious as Atlantis.' He had written to the *Groat* on the subject of Atlantis three weeks before, but so far the editor hadn't seen fit to print it.

Across the road, Jean in the shop was in an ill-naitered mood. She threw the packet of oatcakes onto the counter when Sarah Job remembered she had missed it off her list of messages and Jean had already done the adding up. Miss Job girned a bit at the thought of broken oatcakes but said nothing.

'And that chiel – fat d'ye call him – Dreep,' went on Jean, punching the till buttons fiercely. 'He was that cheeky, impudent and impertinent, coman in here without as much as an excuse me and demandan I get the bobbies. Good mind til get the bobbies til him. Good mind til report him.'

'Oh, weel . . .' said Miss Job as she picked up her slightly battered oatcakes and put them in her bag.

The bell above the door broke merrily into life. Jean shot a red-hot glance to see who this might be bothering her now. The stranger was a tall man of indeterminate age, with a revvle of dark hair above thick glasses. After inspecting his face, both Miss Job and Jean glanced at his feet. He had two.

'Well?' growled Jean.

'Ladies,' said the newcomer. 'Have either of you heard about this foot at the harbour?'

'More than enough,' said Jean, completely drowning out Miss Job's 'Oh weel'.

'Aye?' The man's glasses twitched upward on his nose and settled again. 'What do you think of it?'

'Oh weel . . .' began Miss Job.

'Not a lot,' interrupted Jean. 'It's a bliddy piece o nonsense, if ye ask me. What sensible person would go pittan a perfectly good feet in a bin, especially one o their own?'

'The man must be wounded,' offered Miss Job at last. 'There must have been an accident.'

The stranger had taken out a notebook and was scribbling in it. He paused and looked at Miss Job. 'Is that what you think?'

'Are ye a bobby?' asked Jean.

'Sorry,' said the man. 'No, my name's Alecker Munro. Freelance journalist. I'm covering this story. Gauging the reaction of the village to this amazing turn of events.'

*　　*　　*

Dougie was strolling through one of his parks, deep in a dwaum. He could still mind the day when he had met Alison, over there at the other end of this very park, when he had been dosing sheep for worms and she had come down from the hill where she had been walking. Was that really five years ago? Since then his mother had died and Alison had moved in with him. She had set up her pottery workshop in the old stable, complete with kiln, which had proved a bit hard on the electric bill, though he didn't grudge a penny of it, especially after she began to sell pots to big shops in the south at prices he could hardly believe.

Then they had started a bed and breakfast together, and had built an extension on the old crofthouse. He still carried on some traditional crofting but all in all they had formed a successful partnership with plenty of diversification to keep them in comfort. Now she had agreed to marry him. He knew that he should have asked sooner. The bairn would be born in seven months' time and they had yet to fix a date for the wedding.

Boy or girl? Loonie or lassagie? He wondered but didn't really mind.

*　　*　　*

Alecker Munro left the village shop only partly satisfied. The two women he had met there had not been very helpful and one, the shopkeeper, had made it very clear she thought the whole business of the boot to be nothing but nonsense. He needed something more before he could sell a feature article.

He paused on the pavement and wondered where he could try next. Across the road stood the Brimster Arms. The pub would be worth a visit. Alecker hitched his glasses up on his nose and strode towards it. A promising figure emerged from the public bar – a tall, thin, elderly man. 'Hello,' he called.

The man stopped and waited for him to approach and put the question.

'Ah well, now,' said the tall man. 'That's a question, right enough. It's a deep and mysterious mystery. Do you think it might be a murder? You'll be a detective?'

Alecker explained he was a freelance journalist and, on hearing this, the other man looked at him with renewed interest. 'I can't enlighten you about the boot,' he said, 'but you will be interested in something different. You see, I've just posted a letter to the *Groat* with an amazing discovery I've made. Tell me, does your bed lie north–south?'

Alecker stopped dead. Sinclair Cattach went on: 'You see, if your bed lies north–south rotation will act on the body fluids with equal force throughout and you'll sleep sound and arise refreshed. It's a pity I didn't meet you sooner as that would be a scoop for you. But the *Groat* has beaten you to it. I've just posted them a letter. I can see the disappointment on your face. Don't worry. Here's another one for you that the *Groat* doesn't want. Maybe it's too intellectual for them. You'll have heard of Atlantis?'

Cattach didn't wait for Alecker to answer but went on, gripping the journalist now by the arm so that he couldn't escape. 'You see, I think Atlantis, the mythical land that sank in the Atlantic, is no myth at all. I think it lay between Dunnet Head and the island of Hoy, and you could find it now below the Pentland Firth. D'ye no want to make notes?'

'Eh no, not just now,' stammered Alecker.

'Okay,' went on Cattach. 'If my theory's right, the last bit of Atlantis still showing above the surface is nothing other than the island of Stroma. Not that I'm saying that the Stroma folk were descendants of the inhabitants of Atlantis, no, I'm not saying that at all, that would be going too far, but just the island itself, that's the last bit.'

'I must be going,' cried Alecker frantically, and he tore himself free and hurried off down the street, Cattach shouting after him what sounded like an address and an invitation to drop in for a dram and more information.

After a hundred yards or so, he found himself near the school. Bairns were playing in the yard and two boys lounged at the gate. They were watching him curiously and he stopped to speak to them, savouring the prospect of deploying his old trick of finding out what adults were thinking by interviewing their offspring.

'What's your names?' he asked them.

'Billy,' said one, a tubby peedie chiel with red hair and freckles. 'And he's Gavin.'

'Well, Billy and Gavin,' said Alecker, reaching into his pocket for his notebook. 'Have you heard about what was found at the harbour this morning?'

'No,' said Billy.

He's lying, thought Alecker. 'Sure?'

'Come on, Billy,' shouted Gavin, thin, brown-haired. 'Run.'

Before Alecker could stop them, they darted back in through the school gate. The journalist swore and stared after them. They ran a short distance and then the one called Gavin stopped. 'It wisna us!' he shouted, before resuming his dash after his pal.

*   *   *

Alison dusted and rearranged the pots displayed on the shelf in her studio. Tourists sometimes dropped by to watch her throw a pot and from time to time bought one of them. It was only a small source of income, the main outlet for her work being stores in the south, but it was welcome and she enjoyed talking to the visitors.

She looked at the wheel on which she moulded the pots and thought that, as the baby grew, she might have trouble getting close enough to it. The idea made her smile. The prospect of motherhood was not unwelcome. Dougie had seemed pleased and now plans for the wedding were already forming in her mind. Of course it would change things a bit, being a mother and having a little one to look after, but somehow it seemed to make what had happened to her during the last five years complete.

It had been that long ago that she had left London to find a better life in the countryside. There had been no intention to come so far north – that had been an accident, a happy accident. She had met Dougie and that was something she had never regretted.

Of course, she was seen as an outsider – always would be – but as the partner of a local she was accepted. Now she could understand without too much difficulty what everyone said and knew most of the time how to interpret the nuances in their speech. She doubted if anyone called her a white settler or an ethnic, and making pots might have led readily to her being dubbed a hippy, a word still curiously in use among the older villagers.

The face of Annabella the goat suddenly appeared like a bearded ghost at the window. 'Don't eat those flowers,' shouted Alison. She put down the duster and came out to ensure the goat hadn't already done just that.

Relieved to see the Livingstone daisies she had carefully tended were still safe, she shooed Annabella back towards the byre. Dougie must be out in the fields somewhere. Then she heard the snarl of a car engine and glanced towards the road that ran past their croft to the edge of the hill.

It was a white car, travelling altogether too fast for being on single track. Strangers, tourists, maybe someone seeking bed and breakfast? No, the car didn't slow down but roared on past towards the hill.

'That's odd,' she thought. 'I could swear that was a police car.'

*   *   *

Dougie drove down to the village to buy some messages, musing over what the bobbies could be after in the hill. He slowed as he approached the main road and then crossed it to park outside the Brimster Arms. Bess the collie sat, as she usually did, on the passenger seat of the van, watching the scene unfold. Well used to the ways of her master, she curled up and prepared to wait for his return from the pub.

The sound of a bell came faintly down the street. Two o'clock. Classes were resuming in the school. Dougie called 'Fine day' to the passing Miss Sarah Job and went into the bar. One man – stout and balding – sat before a pint glass.

'Aye John,' said Dougie.

'Aye, Dougie, fit's doan e day?' said John Campbell.

'E usual.' He decided it wasn't yet time to let them know that he and Alison intended to marry.

'It's no your feet then,' added John.

Dougie thought he might have misheard but before he could speak Margaret Manson, the landlady, appeared behind the bar and reached for a glass to pull him a pint. 'Well, he's walkan all right,' she said with a grin as the beer flowed.

'Fit's goan on?'

Sinclair Cattach made his way down the long flight of steps to the harbour. The boats were in. The *Girl Ina* rocked peacefully in her berth and there was no sign of Wildy Ham, her owner and skipper. Astern of her lay the *Polaris*, also appearing deserted. Cattach knew that the day's catch would have been long since stowed in the keep creels where the fishermen held their crabs and lobsters until they went off to the market. Cattach wondered for a moment if shellfish could suffer from boredom, decided that they probably didn't have the brains for it, and picked his way along the quay past the *Polaris*.

A gush of water suddenly spurted from her bilge, spreading little oily rainbows on the sea. There was a loud curse and then the rotund figure of Bowser Clett, fisherman, rose backward like a woolly walrus from the depths of the wheelhouse. As the man's head emerged, Cattach saw that the bonnet was squint and that Bowser himself was sucking the knuckles of his right hand. 'Bliddy pump!'

'She catched ee?' asked Cattach.

'Took a piece oot o me.'

'Seawater's clean,' said Cattach, watching with interest the thin red trickle on the back of Bowser's hand. 'Anyway, I've something I want til discuss with you.'

'Fit?'

'Can I come aboard?'

'No,' said Bowser quickly. 'Wait ere til I come ashore. E last time ee wis aboard ee nearly fell in and I'm no takan e responsibility.'

*   *   *

John Campbell grinned at Dougie as the crofter carried his pint across from the bar and sat down beside him. John winked at Margaret. 'Tell him,' she said.

'Tell me what?' asked Dougie.

'What size o boot d'ye take?'

'Is iss a wind up? I'm no in e mood.'

'No, it's e truth, boy,' said John. 'E scaffies found a boot in e bin at e harbour iss mornane, and there wis a feet in it.'

'It is a wind up.'

'No, it isna,' said Margaret, 'and ee missed all e excitement. E bobbies were here, askan everybody, and we had a reporter in.'

'Was it a livan feet?' Dougie realised how ridiculous was that remark as soon as it left his lips. 'I mean I ken it's deid now, but . . . ye ken fit I mean.'

'Nobody knows far it came fae, or fa it belongs til, or anything,' said John. 'It's a total mystery, as Cattach would say.'

'Did say,' added Margaret. 'That was his very words fan he was in here short ago.'

'He'll dream up some scheme til explain it,' said John. 'That man's brain is fertile enough til grow tatties if ee could plant one in his lug.'

'How's Alison?' asked Margaret.

'A feet. On its own,' mused Dougie. 'Oh she's fine. Radiant.'

John Campbell froze, his pint half way to his mouth. Margaret stopped wiping the counter. They looked at each other. Neither had ever heard the word 'radiant' spoken that way before, at least by Dougie. Oblivious to their curiosity, the crofter drank his heavy and rolled a fag.

The door opened and a man came in. They all greeted him – 'Aye, Bob' – and he grunted in response, a frown on his face. Short Bob – so called to distinguish him from his brother, Lang Tam – had a croft at the edge of the hill. He hoisted his bulk onto a stool at the bar and said he would have a nip.

John Campbell spoke up: 'Have ye heard aboot iss feet, Bob?'

Short Bob swivelled slowly with the help of his elbows to face the two men across the room. 'Heard aboot it?' he repeated sourly. 'Ye can say I've heard aboot it all richt. It's mine.'

Dougie, John and Margaret stared at the squat form of Short Bob, hunched on the bar stool like a defiant gnome. They noticed the dirt on his bonnet, the holes in his gansey and the clay on his boots, both boots.

'Bob,' John Campbell broke the spell. 'My sicht mayna be fit it once was but I can see ye're wearing two boots and conclude that ye've got a feet inside each one. How can the feet in the wheelie bin belong til ee?'

Bob swivelled slowly to pick up his nip of whisky. 'Aye, it's mine all richt. I found it.'

'Where?' asked Margaret.

'In e hill, of course,' growled Bob. 'Fan I was cuttan e peat bank til let watter run off. There was a body buried in e peat, a whole body, I suppose, but I didna dig e whole thing oot. Just up til e knees.'

'It was a deid feet,' said Margaret.

'Of course it was deid. D'ye think I'd take a livan feet off some chiel?'

'I've heard o bodies bein found in peat bogs,' said Dougie. 'The moss can preserve them for hundreds o years.'

John Campbell shook his head in disbelief. 'They told me there was bleed runnan oot o it.'

'Mossy watter maybe,' said Short Bob.

He went on to explain how he had found the body on Saturday but didn't bother to phone anyone at the time. 'I was goan til report it on Monday,' he protested, as if he made such a discovery every day. 'It wasna as if it would go away. If the beggar's been deid for hunders o years, he could surely wait two days. But it turned up in e bin at e harbour seemingly and Dreep phoned e bobbies.'

'How did it get ere?' asked Margaret.

*   *   *

As Short Bob and the others considered who could have stolen a fossilised foot, Jean in the shop across the road was chewing over a grievance. Jess Toft had sailed into the shop to demand a fresh copy of her daily paper because the first one she'd bought had had grease smeared across the front page. 'I'm no payan for damaged goods,' Jess had flyted, 'and it smells o fish as weel.' Jean had had to give her another copy and had thereby lost 40 pence.

'It's that chiel Dreep's fault,' snarled Jean. 'Coman in here til get me til phone e bobbies and pittan his filthy arms on the merchandise. I warned him.'

She looked at the phone for a long moment while she

considered how she might complain to the Council about him. 'Aye, I did warn him,' she said aloud, and reached for the handset.

*   *   *

'Sinclair, ye're fill o damn queer ideas,' said Bowser Clett, as he and Sinclair Cattach walked up the quay from the harbour. 'But I've never heard one like that before.'

'It's a good one, though, you must agree,' urged Cattach. 'And you'll . . .' The sentence remained unfinished as, at that moment, the speaker stepped on a skate gump and nearly fell as it skited away from him.

'Watch your feet,' said Bowser. 'Ye're that fill o ideas, ye canna see far ye're steppan. Last week, ye were wantan me til sail ee ower til Stroma so ee could look for Atlantis.'

'Aye, well,' murmured Cattach. 'That can wait. Now, what aboot giving it a try?'

'Crab-ranching! I've never heard o any chiel doan that.'

'You'd be a pioneer, Bowser.'

'Bliddy laughing stock.' The fisherman paused. 'Ye havna mentioned iss til Wildy, have ye?' Wildy Ham was the other full-time fisherman working out of Brimster and there was a certain rivalry between them.

'Ye're the first, Bowser,' smiled Cattach. 'Ye and me, boy, we go back a long way.'

'I dinna ken.'

*   *   *

Dougie and Short Bob left the pub together. 'I'd like til see iss body ee found,' said Dougie.

'Aye, come ower. E Council chiel, e scientist mannie was oot. I thocht he would hurt himsel wi excitement. E bobbies had realised what it was. No suspicious circumstances, they said. And then they asked me did I want til report a theft? No, as long as we got e feet back, I said, and it wasna damaged, weel, no more than ee'd expect.'

'Fa took it fae e hill?'

'I dinna ken,' said Short Bob. 'If I thocht there would be iss fuss, I'd have covered e beggar up again.'

'Well, I'd better get iss messages and get home,' said Dougie. 'Lamb sale coman up.'

'I hope we get better prices than last year,' were Bob's parting words.

*　　*　　*

There was one man in Brimster that day who knew who might have stolen the foot – Alecker Munro, freelance journalist. As Dougie entered the shop, he was sitting in his parked car, talking on his mobile phone to an editor.

'Aye, I've got a lead,' he was saying. 'Give me a couple of hours – no, one hour at the most – and I'll have the whole story for you. You did say the front page? Oh come on, this is sensational. No, I know it's not a murder. Well, not recently. Look, I'll call you back. One hour.'

Alecker approached the school with a determined, news-hungry look on his face. It was hard enough finding stories in this part of the world, and harder still convincing editors to run them, but surely one would like this. The door was open. As he stepped inside, savouring the whiff of polish, a woman in a pink overall emerged from a side room pushing a trolley laden with plates and cutlery.

'Is the headmaster available?' he asked.

'He'll be in the class just now,' said the woman. 'Have ye an appointment?'

'Eh no, but it is urgent and it'll just take a minute.' It'll take more than that, thought Alecker, but fibbing didn't bother this knight of the press corps. 'And what's your name?'

'They all call me Shirley.' And Shirley eyed the journalist suspiciously. The uncut hair, the thick glasses, the jacket that hadn't seen an iron since it had been bought from a charity shop all marked Alecker in her eyes as a chancer. Which wasn't far off the mark. Shirley, however, was fond of chancers – she'd married one – and she asked him to wait while she went off to get Mr Gill.

*　　*　　*

'Ye see, I've been working it out,' said Sinclair Cattach, as he led Bowser Clett the fisherman into his living room.

Bowser had not been in Cattach's house for some time but it looked exactly as before – the table a mess of papers, probably hiding unwashed plates and half-empty cups of coffee long gone cold, maybe even mice. Some pictures of Cattach's forebears hung around the walls in the gaps between old furniture.

'Sit down,' invited Cattach, but as Bowser began to lower himself into a battered armchair he was halted midway by an ominous growling. 'Just shove the cat oot the road,' said his host. Bowser did not like cats in any shape or form, and the monster in the chair embodied the worst of the species – a muckle, tabby brute with glowering, yellow eyes. Bowser chose to sit in an upright chair at the table, where he had to clear aside only some unprotesting magazines.

'I reckon you can ranch crabs,' went on Cattach. 'Now at present, as you know, you are a hunter, Bowser. The greatest step in the evolution of mankind was the transformation from hunter to farmer. I think it's time you embarked on that step.'

'Ye're talkan rubbish,' said Bowser, 'and ye promised a dram.'

Cattach opened a press and, after sorning in its dark innards, turned round with a bottle of malt in his hand. 'Na, na, it's no rubbish. A prophet is never welcome in his own country, I ken. See that paper there.'

'There's naethane but papers on iss table.'

'Aye, well. I'll show ye. I'll just get a couple of glesses.'

*　　*　　*

Alison stared uncomprehendingly when Dougie stuck his head round the kitchen door and asked her if she wanted to see a body. 'An ancient body,' he added. 'In e hill. Short Bob's.'

'I know Short Bob is knocking on, but I wouldn't call him ancient. And I didn't know he'd died. I don't understand.'

'Bob's still til e fore. I'll explain as we go. We'll no be long but ye'd better get an anorak. It micht rain.'

24

*　　*　　*

Donnie Gill, the headmaster, was suspicious of Alecker but, like Shirley, he was curious and agreed to help him. When the journalist asked for two boys called Billy and Gavin, he brought them to his office, bade the rest of the class get on quietly with their work, shut the door to make it harder for Shirley to hear what was going on, and settled with his backside on the window radiator to observe.

Donnie Gill had spent a good deal of his childhood in Brimster, as his grandparents had lived and died here, and he had come north to fill the headmaster's job with great anticipation and perhaps the teacher's secret wish of nurturing a genius. So far none had appeared. He knew that neither Billy Ham nor Gavin Leavad was going to be a genius, but they were clever and were now eyeing Alecker Munro with all the cunning of their eleven years.

'I know what happened,' Alecker was saying, 'but to save time I'll give you the scenario, and you can correct me if I'm wrong. Okay?'

Billy and Gavin remained impassive.

'Right,' went on Alecker. 'You're playing on the moor and you find something really weird – I mean, far-out weird. In your case, a human foot in a boot, and you don't know what to do. But after a while you take it and put it in a bin at the harbour. Is that familiar?'

Gavin said nothing. The headmaster realised he was waiting for Billy to speak.

'I want you to take me to where you found it,' said Alecker.

'Will we be on the TV?' asked Billy.

*　　*　　*

The last stretch of the road leading to Short Bob's croft was rough and potholed, and the van bounced savagely. In the back, Bess the collie, standing with her four legs braced for the shocks, was better off than the two humans in front.

'I'm going to be sick soon,' cried Alison.

25

'Ye're no, are ye?' said Dougie.

'If there's much more of this I couldn't guarantee anything.'

'It'll no hurt e bairn? I keep forgettan ye're expectan.'

'We're expecting,' corrected Alison. 'It's yours as much as mine.'

'We're nearly there. The road's a bit like Short Bob himsel. Nothing that's no strictly necessary. See the whins.'

The crofthouse ahead of them seemed surrounded by spiky bushes, out of which protruded here and there the corners of abandoned vehicles and the odd discarded household appliance.

'Nae wonder they call iss place Whin City,' laughed Dougie.

A gap in the palisade of thorns appeared at the last moment as the track slewed to an end near Bob's porch.

'Aye,' said Bob, ambling over as they got down. 'It's no far til e bank. I can gie ye a lift.'

He invited them to sit on a wooden plank tied across the back of his Fergie tractor, gave Alison a rolled-up tattie bag as a cushion, and climbed laboriously into the driving seat. 'Haud on,' he shouted, as the tractor lunged forward. The hill road was worse than the one they had already travelled on. It climbed up from the back of the house between parks and more thickets of whins. The passengers hung grimly to the mudguards. 'I spent half e time in e air,' Dougie said later.

The landscape of Brimster opened out around them as they rose to the height of the hill. Alison tried to take her mind off the lurching and the blows to her backside by admiring the pattern of fields and homes, and the sea away to their left with the surf breaking white on the Tangs. Dougie half-turned so he could see ahead and anticipate the biggest bools and deepest holes in their path.

'I hear e Big Hoose is still on sale,' he shouted, as the distant roof of the mansion came into view.

'Heard naethane,' said Bob. 'Maun be.'

'Ere's e bank,' he shouted.

They stopped on a soft bit of peaty road, clambered down and stumbled across the moss. The trench of the bank lay filled with dark water but at the end there were signs of considerable tramping and a tent-like affair of plastic sheeting creaked in the wind.

'E archaeologist mannie covered it all ower,' explained Bob.

'Should we disturb it?' asked Alison.

'We'll no hurt it,' grunted Bob and with a swackness belying his bulk and generally slow movements he jumped across the trench to land beside the tent. Immediately he began to peel aside the plastic. 'See.'

Dougie helped Alison down from the back of the bank and they peered inside the tent. Two dark, stick-like objects protruded from the peat; one ended in a boot, shrunken, black and greasy, and the other ended in what resembled a leathery wad.

'At's e feet at turned up at e harbour,' said Bob helpfully. 'If ee look up along e side, ee can see e mannie's troosers. E peat has preserved e whole thing.'

The visitors stared at the remains in amazement, thoughts of what it all might mean churning through their heads.

'How long do they think he's been there?' asked Alison.

'Naebody kens,' said Bob. 'Twa hunder year, maybe more. He's just pickled in e moss. They're coman back e morn til dig him oot. E archaeologist was ower e moon, beside himsel, poor mannie.'

'I bet it made his year,' agreed Alison.

Dougie stepped back from gazing at the legs. 'He micht be

one o our own folk. I could be lookan at what's left o my umpteen-great grandfaither. I wonder fit his face is like.'

'Oh don't,' cried Alison. 'He might have died in pain. I'll let somebody else uncover him.'

Suddenly they became aware of voices, distant but growing louder, intruding on their reverie. Looking up, they saw two men and two boys coming across the hill towards them. Dougie recognised one of the former as Donnie Gill the teacher, the two boys as Wildy Ham's young chiel, Billy, and Gavin Leavad, and the other man was familiar but he couldn't put a name to him. He didn't have long to dwell in ignorance.

'Aye,' shouted the stranger, striding ahead of his followers. 'Alecker Munro. Journalist. I see you've found the body as well.'

Short Bob drew himself up to his full height, which wasn't much to start with and was even less now that he was slowly sinking in soft moss. 'Fit d'ye mean as weel?'

Alecker seemed not to hear and turned to the boys. 'I want you to stand one on either side of it, and Mr Gill behind, so I can get a picture. We'll need to shift that plastic stuff.'

'Ye said there would be TV,' protested one of the boys.

Short Bob was annoyed by the sudden activity. 'Haud on, haud on a meenad,' he cried. 'Fit's goan on here?'

Alecker paused in his self-appointed task of rearranging the plastic sheeting over the pair of brown shanks sticking out from the peat. 'I want to get a photo of the two boys beside the body. For my story. This'll be all over the country.'

With a great squelch and a visible effort, Bob stepped out from the mossy hole into which he had been slowly sinking and, regaining his dignity along with five inches of height, protested. 'It's my body,' he shouted. 'If anybody's goan til be in e papers, it's goan til be me. It's me fa fand it.'

Billy and Gavin looked unhappy, though whether this condition stemmed from the absence of television cameras or from guilt was uncertain. Dougie and Alison were nonplussed but watched with interest. Donnie Gill decided it was time he sorted the whole mess out. 'Let's take this fae the top,' he suggested.

*   *   *

Bowser Clett tipped back his head and emptied the last drops of Sinclair Cattach's malt whisky on to his tongue. He swallowed, breathed out deeply, tilted forward again in the chair and put the glass down on the table on the only clear spot he could see among the sprawl of papers.

Cattach, who had already poured him two drams, had decided that a couple was enough at this time of day. He had corked the bottle again and had moved it to the other side of the table where Bowser could reach it only by a very obvious stretch. The fisherman felt inhibited from doing this and turned his attention back to what his friend was saying, insistently and in more or less standard English as was his habit when an idea was birling in his brain.

'See,' urged Cattach. 'What you want is a cage like this, lying on the bottom, where you can feed them.'

'Ye canna keep crabs in a cage,' remonstrated Bowser.

'Have you tried?'

'Weel, no, but everybody kens ye canna.' Drawing a living from the sea as he had done all his life had made Bowser sceptical. Innovations were all very well but they usually cost a lot of money and nine times out of ten they didn't work anyway – with Cattach's ideas, the chances were more like ten times out of ten.

'They move intil deep watter in e back end,' said Bowser. 'If ye keep them in one place, they'll pine and dee.'

Cattach looked up with a sly smile. 'I've thocht o that too,' he said, slowly for emphasis.

Bowser sighed, glanced at the malt – out of reach when he seemed to need it most, and began desperately to think of something, anything, at home that might urgently demand his presence.

*   *   *

'So, that's that,' concluded Donnie Gill, as they wandered away from Short Bob's peat bank. The boys had been given a good ticking-off and now seemed relieved nothing worse was coming their way; in fact, they felt proud that they had had their photo taken beside the corpse and looked forward to seeing themselves in the papers. Alecker and Short Bob were following slowly, the journalist scribbling Bob's opinions in his notebook and trying not to trip over heather busses as they went. 'Some carry on, eh?'

'Certainly was,' agreed Dougie. 'Best bit o excitement all week.'

'I'm glad I wasn't in the photo,' added Alison.

At last, under the headmaster's methodical quizzing, the story had been pieced together. Short Bob had found the body and had left it with the feet sticking out. Billy and Gavin had come across it while testing a new bike on the hill tracks. Billy had thought it would be a good idea to pull the strange object from the peat, but the one foot he had heaved on had come off in his arms. Scared, the boys had taken it with them back to the village but had not known how to dispose of it until they had remembered the wheelie bin at the harbour. And then, the next morning, Dreep had opened the lid to find it.

'Do you mind if we walk to the van?' asked Alison. 'I don't think I could endure another ride bouncing on the back of Bob's tractor.'

Donnie went with them until they reached a fork in the track down to Whin City. Here the path to where the journalist had left his car diverged from the route of the others. They stood for a few minutes, discussing the possible history of the poor chiel whose body had lain in the peat for such a long time.

'Well, one good thing is that it micht make the youngsters sit up and take an interest in their history,' said the teacher.

'Aye,' said Dougie. 'Well, we'd better be gettan home. I've got til spend the lambs for the sale.'

'I wonder if we'll ever find out who it was,' said Alison. 'What's his face like?'

*   *   *

Bowser's wife, Isobel, was not too pleased when her man came home from Cattach's house smelling of whisky before his tea. The fisherman didn't tell her he would have taken more if it had been on offer and instead described how Cattach had been blethering on about crab-ranching.

'That man gets ideas like a dowg gets flechs,' said Isobel. 'Last week he wis tellan Jess Toft she should fit a wind generator til her whirligig washane pole. Crab-ranching? I've never heard o at. Fit does he ken aboot at?'

Bowser gave a non-committal grunt. He readily admitted his friend's ideas were often outlandish – to his face, he was in the habit of saying they all were – but from time to time he felt secretly that the old chiel might be on to something. 'We'd need til get some stuff til try it,' he said.

'And fa's money is it goan til be?'

Bowser said nothing.

October

Dreep was unhappy. In fact he had taken deep umbrage. His companions on the Council scaffie round could see this as they sat over their pints in the Brimster Arms.

'Ach, never mind the ould bee,' said Pogo, making another roll-up.

Lang Tam was less sympathetic. 'I warned ye no til go lookan in wheelie bins,' he growled. 'Wir job is just til empty them. It's none o wir business fat fowk pit in them.'

Pogo had a thought. 'Fit if it was a bomb?'

Lang Tam snorted. 'Fit d'ye mean a bomb? It was a deid feet. Fa wid be workan wi bombs in Brimster?'

'Jean had no richt til do it,' Dreep said at last, with a firmness of tone that drew the others' attention instantly. 'She's blackened my name.'

'Weel ye did blacken her papers,' Lang Tam pointed out.

'Imagine,' cried Dreep. 'She phoned wir boss in e Council and telt him at I had damaged her stock and at I should be disciplined and at I should compensate her for her loss. It's defamation o character.'

Lang Tam was not convinced. 'I dinna ken. Have ye got a character?'

'It's libel, at's fit it is,' said Dreep. 'I think I'll sue her for defamation. See how she leks at.'

*   *   *

The lamb sale had been a disappointment but not as big a disappointment as Dougie had feared. Last year had been a disaster. The buyers had kept their hands deep in their pockets and lambs, good lambs, had fetched ridiculously low prices, on the worst occasions less than a pound each.

'A bittie better than last year,' Dougie had commented, when the auctioneer had finally slapped his notebook on the desk and reached the end of the bidding on the crofter's animals. The bigger yowe lambs had been bought for £27 which just about made the enterprise worthwhile. He had kept a handful of poor craiturs back to see if they would put on some more flesh but, as Murdoch Ure said when they met among the mart pens, 'At's it for anither year.'

'I did no bad,' said Dougie.

Murdoch had the farm of Meldale, the biggest place in Brimster. 'Aye, they're clamberan back up slowly, the prices,' he said. 'I think I micht escape a loss this time. How are ye doan? Ye're lookan well.' This last to Alison, as she came to join them.

'I feel fine,' she said.

Dougie coughed. 'Oh Murdoch,' he said shyly. 'I micht as weel tell ye now, before ye hear it fae ithers. We're thinkan o hevan a wedding.'

The farmer's lean face broke into a smile. 'Well at's something. At's good news for once. Fit hev ye done, Alison, til tie him doon?'

She blushed a little but refrained from saying she was pregnant. She didn't really need to as the farmer had spotted the red in her cheeks and reached his own conclusion. 'I'll be lookan oot for an invite,' he said.

'Actually,' said Dougie. 'I wis wonderan if a barn dance micht be . . .'

Alison looked at him sharply, 'You never said.'

'No,' he admitted. 'It was just an idea.'

*   *   *

Alison was still musing over the implications of a barn dance as they drove home. 'We haven't fixed a date yet,' she argued, 'and by the time of the wedding I might be as big as a heifer. I think I'd prefer a quiet wedding.'

'Aye, the wedding can be quiet enough,' agreed Dougie. 'But I think fowk'll expect a party o some kind. I could see Murdoch was taken wi the idea. He has plenty o steading and would be happy til lend e use o a barn. Our own place is too small.'

'Maybe,' said Alison. 'But we need to fix a date.'

*   *   *

They spread out the calendar and a diary on the kitchen table. 'Can we no put it off til efter e New Year?'

'No,' said Alison, firmly. 'I'm not standing in front of the minister with a tummy like a balloon.'

'No, maybe that wouldna look so richt,' mumbled Dougie. 'Weel, it canna be in October. At's too soon. It'll be dark early in November.'

'So what? We'll not be outside. Does it have to be a Friday?'

'Seems so. At's fit folk like. But no e thirteenth. And it'd better no be e weekend o e Armistice.'

'What about December? Early in December, well before Christmas?'

'E coos'll be in.'

Alison wasn't sure how important that was. 'There aren't many weekends left. Does everybody getting married have this problem?'

'We'll hev til see fan e hotel can take us as weel?'

*   *   *

Shirley the school dinner lady was in the shop with a mournful expression on her face, watching Jean, behind the counter, totting up the price of her messages. 'It's my left leg that was the worst,' Shirley was saying. 'The doctor said that he'd never seen such a bad case of varicose veins.'

'At's five pounds and two pence,' intoned Jean.

'Aye, at's what he said,' went on Shirley. 'It was the worst case he'd ever seen. He said at it was a wonder I was still able to walk. Fit else can ye do, I said, ye've got til keep goan.'

Jean wasn't finished. 'Pan scourers. Sixty-nine pence. At's five pounds and seventy-one.'

'Ten stitches I had.'

'Corned beef. Five pounds – six pounds and twenty-five – at's ten, no, twenty-nine . . .'

'Ten.'

Jean vigorously drew a line under the sum. 'Seven pounds ten pence. I had twenty-five stitches fan I had my appendix oot.'

'I think they micht have til do e ither leg,' said Shirley, slowly opening her purse under the weight of her affliction.

The bell above the shop door jingled as it opened to admit Sinclair Cattach. There was a sly grin on his face. The two women looked at him with suspicion. 'Have ye seen the *Groat* the day?' were his first words.

'Why? Fit's in it?' demanded Jean impatiently. 'Some o us dinna have time til look at a paper during e day. Some o us is workan.'

Cattach emitted a strange, bubbling wheeze. 'Aye, I dare say. Oh well, you'll be havan a look before ye go til your bed.'

As soon as Shirley had hirpled out, still firmly believing that ten stitches' worth of varicose veins outclassed an appendix, and Cattach had retreated to the street with two tins of catfood, Jean whisked open the pages of the paper. Her eye beetled across the headlines, scanned all the pictures and finally homed in on the Letters page.

'Rudeness of shopkeepers,' she read aloud, in alarm and bad temper. She went on reading, muttering to herself, '. . . complaints that trade is falling . . . hardly a surprise . . . customers treated with rudeness . . . accused of damaging goods . . . ' and then there was some tripe about motes and planks in eyes. The letter was signed 'Citizen. Name and address supplied.'

Jean clenched her fists and filled the shop with the noise of paper being crushed, as she looked up and glared out at the street. 'Dreep!' she cried.

*   *   *

By bedtime, Dougie and Alison had agreed on a date for the wedding – the third Friday in November. Alison had begun to draw up a guest list of friends and relatives she wanted to invite from England, and Dougie had phoned the Brimster Arms and the minister to establish the day was all right with them. When these exhausting duties had been completed, they poured and drank a large glass of red wine and retired for the night.

There they were waiting at the kirk door, Dougie and Alison, and none of the guests seemed to want to take their places in the pews so that the wedding could go ahead. Bess was running around the guests, trying to round them up and herd them through the door, like the good sheepdog she was, barking furiously . . .

Dougie awoke from the dream. But the barking was still going on. He stared for a moment at the dark ceiling. He recognised the barking. Bess! Beside him, Alison stirred. 'What is it?' she whispered blearily.

'I don't know. Something's set Bess off. It's nobody at e door iss time o nicht, is it?'

'What time is it?'

'E middle e nicht,' he muttered. 'I'll hev til see.'

Sliding out from under the downie, his feet found their way into his slippers. Upright, he rubbed the drowsiness from his eyes, pulled on a jersey and blundered out into the kitchen. The barking echoed like high-pitched thunder. 'Fit is it, dowg?' he moaned.

Bess stopped barking and began instead to whine and sniff at the base of the back door.

'Okay, okay, shut up,' growled Dougie. Bess stopped whining but continued to paw and snuffle at the door. 'There must be somebody ootside.'

He unlocked the door and couldn't pull it open fast enough for the eager collie. Bess disappeared into the darkness and he stumbled after her in his slippers, shivering in the chill. He hadn't gone five yards before he stubbed his toe on a flowerpot, cursed, hopped, and then felt an urgent need to find the bathroom.

Bess flashed back into the pool of light to see what was keeping her master.

'There's nobody here,' he shouted at her. 'It must have been a fox.'

*   *   *

Alecker Munro was feeling very pleased with himself as he

spooned bran flakes into his mouth. 'Oh aye,' he spluttered into the mouthpiece of the phone. 'Good story. Aye. The body in the bog. Sure, I'll follow it up. You can use the picture too. Great.'

'Are you okay?' The voice of the editor betrayed a momentary and uncharacteristic concern for the wellbeing of his northern correspondent.

'Fine, I'm fine, never better,' cried Alecker, wiping milky flecks of bran flakes from the phone.

'By the way,' went on the editor. 'What's this rumour that Brimster House is for sale?'

'It's been on the market for years,' said Alecker.

'Keep an eye on that place,' said the editor mysteriously and rang off.

*   *   *

By mid-morning, Bowser Clett and Sinclair Cattach were well down the road to Inverness. Berriedale and the Ord were behind them, and Bowser was pleased with the way his van had behaved on the steep braes. It was many a long day since he had driven so far and he couldn't remember the last time he had spent so long in top gear. The engine purred as if it were on holiday.

'We're gettan on fine,' said Bowser. 'We'll be in e toon in time for wir dinner.'

At the helm of a fishing boat, Bowser could have circumnavigated the globe without a second thought. He was less certain of direction on a two-lane blacktop and when, at 35 miles per hour, he came upon a large roundabout he blithely turned right instead of left.

'Ye're going against the sun,' observed Cattach . 'Are ye sure that's right?'

On the grounds that when in trouble the best thing was to keep going, Bowser did just that. 'Look til your side,' he told Cattach. So Cattach looked but, as at half past nine that morning a skorrie had dumped its load on the side window and as so far the forecasted rain had not washed it off, all he saw was a white mist. Then, out of the mist, materialised a large lorry with logs. A horn sounded.

'Hard a port,' shouted Cattach.

The van lurched, bumped, shuddered, bumped some more, and there was the open road ahead of them again.

'Fit was at chiel wantan?' asked Bowser.

'I think he was a little upset at your navigation,' said Cattach. 'D'ye consider the possibility that you micht be going a wee bit on the fast side?'

'We want til get til Inverness e day,' complained Bowser. 'Id's been your idea all along, til get iss stuff we need.'

They heard a sudden howling noise, rising and falling. Bowser glanced in the mirror. 'I think at's e bobbies. Fit are they wantan?'

The police car overtook the van, screeched to a halt in a lay-by, disgorged a dark figure pulling on a chequered cap. This figure promptly signaled to Bowser to stop and hurried over to the side of the van.

'What do you think you're doing?' asked the bobby angrily.

'Now,' began Cattach calmly. 'I see you've got a Gaelic motto on your car there. I don't speak the tongue. Could you be telling me what it means?'

Bowser was explaining that they were driving to Inverness, that, aye, it had been a long time since he'd driven so far south, when the other bobby ambled over from the car. Unlike his irate, younger colleague, this officer of the law had a knowing smile on his plump face. 'Far ee twa fae?' he asked.

Three minutes after the ensuing conversation, Bowser and Cattach were on their way again.

'Fit did he mean, "Twa fishermen fae Brimster – at explains everything"?' asked Bowser.

*   *   *

Dougie stood at the end of the steading, puffing slowly at a fag and looking out across his parks. Bess was sniffing around in a strangely excited way. She's getting the smell of something, thought Dougie, I suppose it could have been a fox, or I wonder if it was a polecat. Annabella the goat bleated on the end of her tether and watched him as he dandered along the fence.

Suddenly he stopped, stood straight. The sheep. There was

something odd, out of place. Quickly he counted them. Then he counted them again. The third time he counted only the lambs, the few he had kept back from the recent sale. To his amazement, he had three more than he expected.

*   *   *

Cattach stood at the keyboard entranced. Bowser was less than impressed by his companion's behaviour and felt uncomfortable in the large, brightly lit shop, surrounded by rows of strange machines.

'Come on, boy,' he boomed. 'Never heid playan wi all at gadgets. We've got a long road home aheid o us. I promised hersel we'd be back before nicht.'

Cattach frowned and delicately poked at the keys. 'Just hold on. This is a fascinating device. I've been wantan til get my hands on one for a long time. You know, I could have fun here.'

A young lad wearing a tie and badge appeared and started to unroll a spiel of information to Cattach. Bowser understood not one word but sensed instinctively that it all boiled down to parting with a great deal of money. When he heard Cattach say 'So I can get email and surf the web with this one,' Bowser knew it was too late and that drastic action was called for.

He grabbed his companion by the arm and, with the strength developed from years of hauling creels, dragged him effortlessly towards the door. 'Now, now, Bowser, steady on,' protested Cattach breathlessly, 'I was only lookan at it. I must get one o them.'

'No e day, you're no. We've got til get home.'

'Have you bocht a present for hersel? You should get her something, a bonny new apron or a bunch o flowers.'

'She's got plenty o aprons and there's flooers in e gairden.'

Cattach shook himself loose from Bowser's clep-like grip. 'That computer was on special offer. It's a chance not to be missed. Time and tide wait for no man. We've room for it in our transport and I'll no be a minute.'

Bowser sighed and looked out to the car park, to where the van sat, a little battered and in need of a wash. They had already bought rope, netting and metal rods, and the fisherman wondered what else would be stowed aboard before they left. 'Hurry up, then,' he muttered.

*   *   *

Dougie closely surveyed his flock of sheep, penned in a corner of the park. Her tongue lolling with exertion and excitement, Bess the collie patrolled the gate in case a bold yowe made a bolt for freedom, while Alison stood watching with her arms folded against the morning chill. 'Are you sure there are too many?' she asked.

'At e last coont I had three too many,' said Dougie. 'And at's them ere. D'ye see at three little chiels?'

'They look awful poor, runty things.'

Dougie waded in among the closely packed animals and

grabbed one. He lifted the lamb in his arms, holding it for Alison's inspection.

'There's no marks on e lugs or on e body.'

'What's that red spot on its head?'

'Just til show it's a wether, I think. We do at wirsels til make it easier til sort them.'

'How did they get here? Have they strayed?'

'Maybe. But there wis all at carry-on last nicht, wi Bess gettan excited. D'ye think somebody micht have put them here?'

Alison shivered and drew her cardigan more tightly about her shoulders. 'I suppose we'll just have to keep them for now. I need to warm up, and we've got an invitation list to draw up.'

The reminder of all that had to be done to prepare for the wedding made Dougie girn. He put down the lamb. 'If we're goan til do at,' he said, 'ye'd better put the kettle on, and put a slug o whisky in e coffee.'

*   *   *

Billy Ham and Gavin Leavad compared what money each had in his pocket. 'I can get five more bangers,' said Billy, totting up the coins in the palm of his hand.

'Or a rocket,' said Gavin. 'We could fire it sideways. Have ye ever done at? It goes off like a missile.'

'My faither says I've got til be in by nine o'clock,' said Billy.

'At's okay, at still gies us plenty o time.'

'Sure?'

'Aye. We can take wir bikes. No lichts on, so nobody can see us in e dark.'

At that moment the school bell burst into loud activity.

'I'm tellan ye,' cried Gavin above the ringing. 'Iss'll be the best Hallowe'en we've ever done.'

*   *   *

'I make it thirty to the ceremony.' Alison set down the pen and sipped her coffee.

Dougie eyed the long list of names she had drawn up. 'Seems

a fair crowd. D'ye think all your relatives'll come up fae England?'

'My mother will. She never misses a wedding. And my sister will come, as she's the bridesmaid. Aunts and uncles – probably not, but they'll be offended if they aren't invited. If they all come, we couldn't put them up.'

'The Brimster Arms may offer a special rate.'

'Now,' said Alison more firmly, 'You must decide on a best man.'

The phone rang before Dougie could think of another excuse for not having carried out this most important duty. When he answered the call, he heard the voice of Murdoch Ure, who farmed Meldale.

'Ah, Dougie,' he heard Murdoch say. 'How are ye doan the day?'

'Fine.'

'Well, I'll tell ye what it is. Are ye missan any lambs at all? I'll tell ye why I'm asking. There's some here in wi my flock at doesna belong til me.'

'It's funny ee should say at, Murdoch . . .' began Dougie.

'I've got four too many.'

*   *   *

Darkness had fallen across Brimster. Alecker Munro peered through the windscreen as he drove up the untarred road in the direction of Brimster House, or the Big Hoose as it was more commonly known in the district. The headlights did not reveal all the potholes in his path and he slowed to save too much stress on the already battered suspension.

The editor had urged Alecker to check out a very interesting rumour that the Big Hoose, a gaunt, former shooting lodge, had been bought at last. The Brimsters, an obscure branch of the Sinclairs, had run out of cash long before the last survivor of the family, an eccentric retired admiral who had been in the habit of taking double-barrelled potshots at skorries, had passed away virtually penniless. Nothing had been done to keep the property in trim since anyone could mind and it was said to be in sore need of renovation.

Alecker winced as the car bounced through another rut and the exhaust struck the ground. At last, mindful of his account with the garage, he pulled into the side of a clump of whins and resolved to go ahead on foot. Fishing a torch from the glove compartment, Alecker set off on the last half mile of his journey.

Away over the village he could see rockets streaming up into the night sky and hear the bangs and whooshes of other fireworks. All the bairns would be out celebrating Hallowe'en and the older people would be watching for mischief. Alecker thought again that it might have been better to leave this expedition for daylight but, if he could steal a lead of a few hours over rivals, the editor would be very pleased indeed and the reward would be all the greater.

Ahead now he could see the black outline of the Big Hoose looming against the sky. And wonder of wonders there was a light in one of the windows. Alecker splashed through a puddle, cursed as cold water soaked through his socks, and hurried on.

*   *   *

'Come on, let's go on for a little bittie.' Gavin was eager and insistent. His pal, Billy, stubbornly said nothing and sat on his bike. The pair had ridden up all the way from the village to Whin City in the darkness, intent on doing something to Short Bob or his property to mark Hallowe'en. But now Billy was thinking better of it.

'We're missan everything at home,' he complained.

'We'll no be long. We could take a gate.'

'On bikes?'

'Well, maybe no. Put a banger in his door.'

Billy was reluctant. 'At's stupid. He's deaf.'

'He's no deaf,' countered Gavin.

'I'm goan back.' Billy turned his bike and set off down the track. Gavin shouted to him to wait and pedalled after him. They came to a fork and in the darkness went some way in the wrong direction before they realised the village seemed to be growing more distant.

'Far are we?' asked Gavin.

'I think I ken,' said Billy. 'See that black shape way ower yonder. At's e Big Hoose.'

'Is it haunted?'

'Dinna ken. E mannie's deid.'

'Let's go and see.'

The boys resumed pedalling and soon came down to another road, wider than the one they were on. Whins grew in large, dark ramparts around them. They turned in the direction of the main road, where they could see the lights of an occasional passing car, and careered on. But they hadn't gone far when they spotted in the beam of their own headlamps a parked vehicle.

*   *   *

Alecker paused as he reached the rickety gate at the Big Hoose. Beyond it he could see a flagstone path winding through untended bushes and long grass. The light shone from one downstairs window but the curtains were drawn and nothing of the interior was revealed. The journalist shivered slightly as the tremulous call of an owl sounded very close but, dismissing from his head all thoughts of evil spirits, he tightened his coat about his neck and pushed open the gate.

It squeaked loudly on the stone but he carried bravely on, trying not to let his feet echo on the hard surface. The door was closed. He switched on the torch to look for a bell but found none. In the centre of the studded, peeling wood hung a knocker in the shape of an eagle's beak.

Instead of using it, he stepped back a couple of paces and called loudly 'Hello. Anybody in?'

Silence for a long moment and then the owl called again.

'Hello,' he shouted again. 'The name's Munro. Alecker Munro. Is there anybody in?'

Then he heard a sound, a sound like a door slamming deep within the dark building. This was followed by silence before a rustling noise suddenly erupted uncomfortably close and he had an impression of a white shape rushing towards him. The white thing hit Alecker in the legs and cowped him. He had a fleeting impression of baaing sounds and of a human voice asking something, and then he passed out. When he came to, he realised he was lying on a couch. His head rested on something soft, probably a cushion, and he thought this was just as well, as a throbbing pain was darting through the back of his skull.

'Can you hear me?'

Alecker opened his eyes. Someone was bending over him, staring with concern at his face. The journalist blinked and focused. The stranger was tall, quite young and powerfully built.

'I saw a ghost,' moaned Alecker.

'I don't know what you saw, mate,' said the stranger, 'but it was a sheep that knocked you over. You've had a pretty bad knock on the head.'

'Sheep?'

'Yeah. They get in through a hole in the wall.'

'I must get til Brimster Hoose.' Alecker sat up with this forceful declaration of intent but the pain in his head was too much to thole and he shut his eyes and moaned.

'This is Brimster House. What we want to know is what you're doing here.'

*   *   *

One hour later, Alecker was stumbling back down the track from the House towards where he had left his car. The sudden flare and fade of fireworks in the village reminded him it was still Hallowe'en, but the dazzle of Roman candles, rockets and Catherine wheels was nothing to the starry enlightenment in his brain. Though it was enlightenment befuddled with two large glassfuls of malt whisky.

Boy, had he a story! A story and a half. The highpoint of his career as a freelancer. In his excitement he punched the air and whooped in the darkness, and in his befuddlement he staggered into some whins and retreated with torn trousers. Who would believe it? After being empty for so long, who should have bought Brimster House but . . . he couldn't bring himself to believe he had met her, had actually shaken her hand, had actually drunk two glassfuls of malt whisky that her minder – nice gadgie, that Trev – had poured for him.

I need a photograph, he thought suddenly. Tomorrow, I'll call tomorrow. Then he saw his car, a black shape looming ahead. In fact, he saw it too late and fell across the bonnet. He groped for his keys, dragged himself round to the door, opened it and fell into the seat. Somehow in the darkness he couldn't find the ignition. Concentrating brought on a fresh wave of the ache in his head and he closed his eyes to relieve it and, unaccountably, fell asleep.

*   *   *

Dougie was feeling pleased with himself. He had fixed the wedding date and time with Mr Milton, the minister; Donnie Gill, the headmaster, had agreed to be his best man, and had gleefully promised a humdinger of a speech (Dougie saw that as a threat but no matter); and the Mansons at the Brimster Arms were already drawing up the menu for the reception. Alison's mother, the widowed Mrs Gladys Trundle, and sister, Michelle, were already planning their trip north. Now all that remained to be done was to pin down arrangements with Murdoch Ure at Meldale for the barn dance.

'This should be big enough,' said Murdoch, as the two of them stood in a clear part of the steading. 'I'll sweep the flags and shift at bags o fertiliser. Ye can set up a bar here on trestles. Fa's doan e music?'

'I've booked Ian Toft and the Northern Lights.'

'All e invitations oot?'

'Oh aye. Alison's seen til all at.'

Murdoch said that was all fine. 'By the way,' he went on. 'I still dinna ken fa at four lambs belong til. Ye said ye've got three strays.'

'I'm no so sure they're strays,' explained Dougie. He told Murdoch how Bess the collie had been excited one night, as if something strange was going on outside, and how he had found the extra lambs the following morning. 'Ye would think somebody put them in my park but so far I'm no further on.'

'We'll get til e bottom o it somehow,' said Murdoch. 'I think we'll need til rig up some kind o heating in here. Maybe an hour wi the corn drier would do the trick.'

'If they're dancan hard enough they'll heat themsels. And there'll be plenty til drink.'

*　　*　　*

Alecker's excitement had metamorphosed into a hangover, and his feet were wet and sore. Waking up in the driving seat of his car just as dawn was breaking over Brimster, he had spent several minutes recollecting what had happened during the night. There was a lump on the back of his head, where he had fallen, but the tenderness there had been nothing to the pulsing throb above his eyes and the dryness in his mouth. And then he had found all his tyres were flat, the result (though he didn't know it) of a Hallowe'en ploy, and had had to walk the Lord knew how many miles to get to the village. He fumbled in his coat pocket for his phone.

*　　*　　*

Sitting on a low dyke beside John Campbell's workshop, waiting for the mechanic to drive him and a pump back to the hill to collect his abandoned car, Alecker was trying to compose a story. When he had his facts straight, he punched his mobile phone.

'Alecker here,' he said, when the editor answered. 'Brimster House. Big news. It's been bought by Amethyst Dean. I'll give you a thousand words by two o'clock. No, I've got no pictures. What? Five hundred words? After what I've been through? What d'ye mean, too bad? It's Amethyst Dean!'

*　　*　　*

'Isn't it exciting? You're going to have Amethyst Dean for a neighbour,' enthused Alison's mother on the way to Brimster. Alison had met her and her sister, Michelle, off the train.

'I suppose so, mother,' said Alison. 'But I don't think she'll overwhelm the locals. I know she's up there somewhere between Madonna and the Spice Girls, with her picture on the front of every magazine, but that doesn't count for everything. We're a canny bunch here, you know.'

'We?' echoed Michelle. 'You count yourself one of them now?'

'Maybe I do,' smiled Alison.

'You've turned Scotch,' cried her mother. 'I always knew you would.'

'Mother, how could you know that?'

'I'm your mother, aren't I?'

Alison slowed to pass through the village. 'You won't embarrass me at this wedding? Promise.'

November

The wedding took place on a bright, cold day. A stiffish wind
swirled around the houses, stiffish, that is, by Brimster standards.
To Alison's mother and sister, it more closely resembled an Arctic
gale, and during the short walk from the car to the hotel Mother
had to hold tightly with one hand to her hat, a wide-brimmed
pale-blue creation displaying an urge to fly to Norway, and with
the other keep her coat and dress from exposing her thighs to the
elements. By the time she staggered through the door she was
quite breathless and had to stand for a moment until the puffing
subsided.

'Aye, it's breezy,' said a tall, thin, elderly man who turned
from leafing through the brochures on a side table.

'Is that what you call it?' wheezed Mother.

'Eh, you'll be Alison's mam,' said the man. 'We've heard all
aboot you. My name's Cattach but you can
call me Sinclair if you like. Have you been
bothered wi tiredness for a while? You see, it
micht help if you shifted your bed . . .'

'You can call me Gladys. It's a drink I
need, beds can come later. Is this the way in?'

＊　　＊　　＊

Alison wore a simple cream-coloured dress,
and Michelle had a similar design in a pale
yellow that complemented her blonde hair.
Dougie had to overcome mild astonishment
when his bride emerged to stand by his side
before Mr Milton, the minister. How had
Alison managed to secure such an outfit

without him even suspecting she might? His own suit – he had resisted the temptation to buy a new one – had been subjected to a grooming and brushing worthy of a prize heifer but still the odd shred or two of fluff worked their way from overlooked hiding places.

The ceremony passed off before the assembled guests without a hitch. Gladys shed a few tears for appearance's sake as her elder daughter tied the knot. Donnie Gill didn't drop the ring at the wrong moment. The lines were said and the vows were made without a stumble, and no one had the bad manners to draw attention to the slight bump in Alison's middle.

With a scraping of chairs that almost drowned the electric organ, ably played by Margaret Manson, the guests made for the bar as soon as the ceremony was complete, to pass the time before they were summoned to dine. Dougie and Alison shook everyone's hand, another scraping of chairs ensued as the guests jostled for their seats, and then the waitresses sallied out from the kitchen with tureens of broth. The rest of the meal followed impeccably until the moment could be put off no longer. Donnie Gill clattered a dessert spoon against a wine glass and when all had turned their heads in his direction he stood and beamed upon them.

'Ladies and gentlemen, Dougie and Alison,' he began in his strong, headmaster's voice. 'Welcome til you all. We've eaten well, we've drank well, and our friends here, Dougie and Alison, have been wedded well. We have a few more formalities to go through before we get doon til serious celebrating. First, I'll call on Mr Milton to say a few words.'

'Oh God,' whispered Dougie to Alison. 'Here we go. Iss is e worst bit.'

'Have you got your speech written?'

'Aye,' he mouthed, and he fished in his pocket. 'I had it here.'

Mr Milton the minister concluded his short address with the toast to the couple, and everyone stood and repeated the words. Alison noticed with a little thrill of alarm that her mother tossed back her whisky in a oner and then called to a waiter for a refill. Dougie was struggling to his feet. 'Eh, ladies and gentlemen,' began her husband.

'Speak up,' came a voice from the other end of the table, to which several others responded with a fierce 'Husht!'

'I hed a speech here somewhere,' went on Dougie, louder, while fishing in his pocket. 'Ah, here it is. It's no long, ye'll be glad til hear.' He unfolded the square of paper and thanked everyone, naming those who had to be named and ending, with a strong feeling of relief, with his toast to the bridesmaid, Alison's younger sister, Michelle. 'At wisna so bad,' he breathed, sitting down again.

The tinkle of a spoon against a glass cut through the scraping of chairs and shuffling of feet, and Donnie Gill rose again. His voice, honed by years in the classroom, cut through the hubbub and commanded attention.

'Now I was greatly honoured when Dougie asked me til be his best man,' he continued, after the usual preliminaries. 'I've never been a best man before, and my wife will vouch for at. Why did Dougie ask me? I wondered aboot at, and the only answer I could come up wi is at I'm a relative newcomer in the place. No a total newcomer, as my grandparents belonged here and I used til come here on my holidays when I was a boyagie. I kent Dougie then. My grandfaither pointed him oot til me – "a grand loon" he used til say – and I'll echo at, and no just because I'm standing here drinking at his expense. No, I think Dougie picked me til be his best man because he thocht I michtna ken too much aboot him. Ah but there ye're wrong, my friend.'

Delighted by this promise of revelation, the guests leaned forward over the crockery or sat back in their chairs to see and hear better.

'It's no too late til sack ye,' cried Dougie.

'Or send you a bill,' added Alison.

'First I have a telegram or two til read,' said Donnie. He picked up the first and scanned it quickly before intoning the message of best wishes, and the announcement of the sender's name set off some murmuring of recognition among the guests. 'And here's one fae some chiel called Gill in Glasgow. It could be my faither. "Congratulations and best wishes. You've a good man there, Alison, dinna wear him oot too fast." And here's one fae Magnus Stroup.'

The announcement of the name of the local councillor caused a stir, but it was hard to tell from the top table whether this signified approval or scepticism.

'"Fertile fields and fruitful flocks",' read Donnie.

'He's efter your vote, Dougie,' called a voice, instantly greeted with laughter.

Donnie finished the telegram reading and returned to his theme – Dougie's early life. He made several references to Hogmanay binges, crop circles, expeditions to fish for cuddanes, and then said he had found an early love letter from Dougie to Alison.

'I never wrote one,' protested the groom.

'Well, if you had done, iss is what you micht have said,' replied Donnie. '"My dearest Alison, Hope you're all richt, Finished liftan e tatties, Did ye find your elastic? I love you, Dougie." So, ladies and gentlemen, we never suspected we had such a romantic, sensitive soul among us.'

*   *   *

Afterwards Alison admitted to her mother that the dinner had passed better than she had feared. 'They can be very earthy, especially some of Dougie's pals,' she said. 'Don't ask me how it feels to be a married woman. I'm just the same.'

'Oh love,' whispered Gladys, too overcome to say more, her lower lip trembling like a birch leaf in a gale. 'It was beautiful. And you were beautiful. And Michelle was beautiful. And I just wish your dad had been here to see you. I'm so happy.' And finally the lip could no longer hold and she burst into tears.

Michelle came bustling in from the bathroom. 'How long do we have to wear these frocks? They don't seem right for a barn dance.'

'Just for the first hour or so,' said Alison, holding a paper hankie for her mother to blow her nose. 'Then we can change. Don't worry, you won't get covered in straw. The place has been cleaned up, or so I'm told.'

'We'd better be off,' shouted Dougie, sticking his head round the door.

Murdoch and Bella Ure had done a great job in preparing their steading, everyone agreed. The bar and the band were in position and all were waiting for the arrival of the couple for the dancing to start. Bowser Clett, however, had a complaint.

'Cattach,' he growled to his companion. 'I wish ye wid shut the dot up aboot that computer o yours. I canna get a word o sense oot o ye since ye got the bliddy thing home.'

'Ah well, you see, you've got til move wi the times.' Cattach was not to be put off. 'Just you wait. It brings the world til our door.'

Pogo and Dreep had managed to wash off the grime acquired in their round on the scaffie cart and now wore their best clothes. 'I'm goan til ask Michelle for a dance,' declared Pogo, his mouth poised over his pint.

'Ye've no chance,' cried Dreep.

'Hev I no?' grinned Pogo in triumph. 'Anyway ye'll be too busy dancan wi Jean fae e shop.'

'I'm no feard o her.'

'We'll see aboot at.'

'Here she comes now.' Pogo chuckled with delight as he said the dreaded words.

'She's no coman ower here, is she?' Dreep had turned his back to the door and couldn't find the courage to look.

'She doesna ken ye in a suit,' said Pogo. 'Ye should hev kept your boiler suit on.'

Dreep turned at last, saw that Jean from the shop had joined a table of friends at the other end of the long barn, and sighed in relief. All the residents of Brimster had been invited to the barn dance and almost all had turned up, including Miss Sarah Job, who now sat among the Hams, apparently enjoying herself with a glass of sherry. Cattach sat with the Cletts, and the Tofts were at the next table and, beyond them, the Leavads and the Campbells. Peggy Stroup and her daughters, Fiona and Catriona, had a table to themselves; her husband, Magnus, agricultural salesman and councillor, was expected along later. Mr Milton the minister and Donnie Gill the teacher were blethering to Murdoch at the last table near the platform, made of bales overlain with duckboards and a tarpaulin, where the band, Ian Toft and the Northern Lights, were playing.

'We've a prominent new parishioner,' Donnie Gill was saying.

'If you're referring to Amethyst Dean, I don't expect to see her in a pew come Sunday,' replied Mr Milton. 'Mind you, if she did come, every youngster in the place would be there at her heel.'

'Not to mention the press.'

'In that case, I might just prefer to make a pastoral visit.'

Muroch Ure shook his head. 'I canna see what all the fuss is aboot. She's just a pop singer. And I canna make heid nor tail o her music.'

'No just a pop singer,' laughed Donnie. 'She's a star.'

'The stars in the Ploo will do me,' said Murdoch.

A commotion at the end of the barn signalled the entry of the married couple and the official start of the proceedings.

*   *   *

'At's e stuff til set your blood racing.' Cattach's comment on the Strip the Willow he had just whirled through seemed hardly an adequate description to Gladys. 'My head's spinning and my feet are throbbing,' she gasped, 'I don't know about my blood, I'm sure. Oh!' And she dabbed at the perspiration on her cheeks.

'It's a drink ye'll be needing,' pronounced Cattach. He shot off through the crowd and returned with two glasses.

'Lord, more whisky,' squawked Gladys. 'Well, I don't know.'

A few yards away, Dreep nudged Pogo. 'D'ye think Cattach's tryan til get off wi e English wifie?'

'Na,' was Pogo's considered opinion. 'He's no her type. See ye!'

'Far ee off . . .?' Dreep darted after his companion and caught up with him just as Pogo reached Michelle. Almost together, the two scaffies yelled, 'D'ye want til dance?'

'You can both dance with her,' cried Alison. 'It's a Dashing White Sergeant.'

*　　*　　*

Dougie collapsed in his chair, loosened his tie and drank deeply from the pint of heavy. 'Bearing up?' asked Alison, arriving to sit beside him.

'So far. How about ye?'

'Getting a bit tired, to tell you the truth. I shouldn't have eaten so much and now the wee one is restless.' She groaned. 'He's kicking.'

'Probably drunk.'

'Don't make me laugh. I'm too sore. What do you say to slipping away soon? Leave this lot to it?'

Which is just what the couple did. Bidding goodnight to all their guests and politely turning down all the proffered drams, Dougie and Alison left the barn dance. Bella Ure volunteered to drive them to their croft, adding that she would make sure Gladys and Michelle eventually reached home safely as well.

As they slid through the night, following the beams of the headlights, rain began to fall. They passed through the deserted village street. 'I think everybody's at e wedding,' commented Bella. The road dipped across the burn by the old mill and rose again towards the edge of the hill.

'E rain's gettan heavier. There's an umbrella somewhere beside ye,' said Bella.

'Never heed,' said Dougie. 'A drop'll no bother us.'

They got out and watched as the car bounced away in the night. Then they paused for a moment, in the lee of the house, and kissed. 'Mrs Bayne, may I have the pleasure?'

'You surely may, Mr Bayne.'

Suddenly there was the scrape of a footstep on the flagstones. The couple leapt in surprise and whirled to see standing in the glare of the light shining from the gable end a figure they recognised simultaneously.

'Short Bob! What the devil are ye doan here?'

An instant after Dougie and Alison saw him, he was no longer there. The gable light shone on empty flagstones.

'That was Short Bob, was it no? What's he up to?' whispered Alison in some alarm.

'Lord kens.' Dougie moved to the edge of the close and called 'Bob!' Then he turned back to Alison. 'He's disappeared.'

They stood for a moment, staring at each other, each hoping the other would provide an answer. The only sounds were the dripping of the rain from the rhones and the faint whisper of the wind. Then they heard a crash, coming from the darkness somewhere behind the steading.

'Wait here,' said Dougie, and he ran off into the night. He paused briefly by the byre until his eyes grew accustomed to the gloom. Rain was now beginning to find its way down his neck, urging him to move.

From nearby came a moan and, peering down, he saw a dark bundle huddled by the drawbar of the baler. 'Bob, is at ee?' More moans. The bundle moved and assumed the shape of a man lying on the ground.

'Come on, Bob. Come intil e hoose. Hev ee hurt yoursel?'

'I've lost all feeling below ma knees,' came the plaintive voice, as Dougie helped the crofter to his feet. Together, they hullupped back to the house. 'Fit is it ye're doan here?'

*   *   *

Back in the barn at Meldale, the wedding dance was still in full swing. Ian Toft and the Northern Lights hammered out the last chords of a waltz and the dancers ebbed from the floor. Gladys found her daughter, Michelle, and dragged her to one side.

'You're enjoying yourself, Mother. Who is that man you've been with?'

'I don't know,' gasped Gladys. 'I think he's simple. He kept telling me all about some place called Atlantis and invited me to go to see it in a boat. At least I think that's what he was saying. I couldn't understand him half the time. I need a drink.'

Pogo and Dreep stood at the bar. Both were now in their shirtsleeves and their ties were askew. 'She's beautiful,' sighed Pogo.

'She'll no look at ee, then,' swore Dreep. 'Ye're just a chuchter. She's sophisticated.'

'I can be sophisticated if I want.'

'Wi half a sausage roll on your chin?'

Pogo wiped away the crumbs and then licked them from the back of his hand, commenting they were 'Bliddy tasty' as the band called for an eightsome reel. Suddenly a hand descended fiercely on Dreep's shoulder. He whirled around to see the grinning visage of Jean from the shop far too close for his comfort. He tried to bolt but the fingers gripping his skinny frame held fast.

'Oh no, I've got ye iss time,' whispered Jean. 'Eightsome reel. Ye're mine!'

Dreep gulped, 'I dinna ken how til do it.'

'Ye'll soon learn.'

Jean dragged her terrified partner on to the dance floor and placed him by her side where he stood like a rabbit caught in headlights. 'Now we'll see fit ye think o shopkeepers,' she declared.

Dreep found his voice but it had a high, tremulous quality that surprised him. 'I didna mean it. It wisna me . . .' but the music and the laughter cut him off, and then he was being dragged in a fast-moving ring of dancers that reversed direction with a force that nearly cowped him.

Jean took the centre first and he knew what was coming, but he was helpless, transfixed before his fate, a grin frozen on his face. The moment came and he and Jean were whirling in the middle of the ring, his arm clenched under her elbow. Faster and faster she spun. Dreep lost track of his bearings, his feet lost contact with the floor, and then he was flying through the air, free as a bird, free – until he crashed backwards into the table where Miss Sarah Job was sipping her umpteenth small glass of sherry.

*   *   *

'I thocht ye widna be back so soon,' said Short Bob, sitting in a disconsolate heap at the end of the kitchen table. 'Och never heid at. It's far fae ma hert.'

Alison had rolled up his trouser leg and was putting a large swathe of sticking plaster on the gash in his shin. 'That should do you,' she said.

'It's the sheep, ye see,' went on Bob, sorrowfully. 'I got such a low price at e sale at I couldna afford til let them go. And I couldna afford til keep them either, hay being e price it is.'

'I get it now,' nodded Dougie. 'Ye gave me three o your lambs, and ye gave Murdoch four. Surely ye kent I would notice?'

'Aye, but I kent as weel at ye widna let them starve, e craiturs. I thocht ye widna mind one more, but ye catched me.'

'Why did ye no ask?'

Bob girned but could not bring himself to admit his pride prevented asking for charity.

'Well, I suppose reverse sheep rustling is something novel,' commented Alison.

*   *   *

'Ye should've seen him,' laughed Pogo, as the three scaffies assuaged their drouth in the Brimster Arms. 'Lyan ere amang e chairs lek a wounded scorrie. Jean threw him across e room lek a bag o manure. We should get her on e round. She could fairly handle wheelie bins.'

'I fell,' cried Dreep, 'and I've still got a bruise on ma backside til prove it.'

Lang Tam grunted and reached for his pint. 'At'll learn ee no til go writan letters til e paper aboot Jean.'

'She was quite good aboot it efterwards.' Pogo grinned. 'Helped him til his feet and dragged him back intil e dance.'

'She nearly murdered me.'

'Ye can buy her a Christmas present,' said Lang Tam.

'Weel, I'll tell ee she disna need a bodybuilding outfit,' said Pogo.

*   *   *

'We can but thank ee for all ye've done, Murdoch, ye and Bella,' said Dougie.

'No bother. It was a good nicht, boy,' agreed Murdoch. 'We got til wir beds at three. And I'm glad we've sorted oot Short Bob. He has a hard trauchle wi that soor ground o his at Whin City.'

'Aye. I said at he could leave his four lambs wi my flock ower the winter, and he's got anither four wi ye. He should get a better price for them in e spring. I telt him he should have asked aforehand and no come smugglan sheep.'

Murdoch nodded. 'Poor mannie, he was embarrassed. Any more word aboot e body he found in e hill?'

'I heard there's goan til be a display o photos in e hall.'

'Good. At'll be interestan, til see fit he looked lek. Your folks all off again?'

'Aye, Alison has run her mother and Michelle in to catch the train. They had a good time, and are sayan they'll be back in e summer.'

*   *   *

'Now you see and keep warm and keep feeding yourself.'

'Yes, mother. I know, I'm eating for two now. You keep telling me. You'd better get a seat.'

Gladys heaved herself aboard the train, following Michelle carrying the suitcases.

'Are you sure you don't want me back when . . . you know?'

'You're always welcome, you know that. But I'll be all right. They have a good hospital here, and Dr Lee's very nice. He's not worried.'

Gladys tilted her head in a gesture of understanding sympathy. 'Oh but it's not the same . . . but if you're sure.'

'Phone me when you get home,' cried Alison, as the station-master signalled departure. The train began to glide slowly forward. Alison waved to her mother and heard a diminishing cry of 'Keep warm.'

*   *   *

Miss Sarah Job examined her reflection in the bathroom mirror. An excess of sherry at the wedding dance had left her feeling very poorly and she felt she was in for a bout of the flu. Tiredness, thirst, attacks of dizziness – and now she could see that her eyes looked very heavy. Jean at the shop had sold her a packet of aspirin, an embarrassing moment as the minister, Mr Milton, had come in for his paper just as Jean was advising her on what to take. Fortunately the minister had not appeared to notice anything amiss – Sarah had breathed away from him just to make sure – and had left again, saying he was going to meet his son off the train.

Sarah decided she should rest and she was beginning to regret she had phoned the doctor when she heard the bell ring. Smoothing her grey hair and her clothes, she hurried to open the door.

'Hello,' said a young man she hadn't seen before. 'Miss Job?'

'Oh weel, yes,' she answered.

'I'm Dr Ball. I'm a trainee with Dr Lee at present. He can't come himself but I hope I'll do.' And he smiled so sweetly, and looked so young and handsome standing on her doormat, that Sarah's hangover disappeared and she opened the door wide.

'Oh doctor, I'm so sorry,' she said. 'It's nothing really, just a wee touch o the cold.'

'Better safe than sorry.' Dr Ball waited for her to close the door behind him. 'I'm here, so I might as well do my job, eh?'

Sarah showed him into the living room and invited him to sit on the couch. He didn't want any tea and proceeded with his examination. He sounded her, looked at her tongue, had her say 'Ah' twice. She told him that she thought she had caught a chill from the damp, cold weather they'd been having and told him coyly that she was no longer as young as she used to be, an observation with which he politely agreed. Then he sneezed.

'Oh mercy, doctor, have I smit you?' she cried in alarm.

'No,' he managed to say, before sneezing loudly again. And again. And a fourth time. Tears were now welling in his eyes and starting to trickle down his cheeks.

'Oh mercy!' cried Sarah.

The young doctor sneezed again with a great roar and a violent spasm that shook his whole body, throwing his feet into the air. Sarah forgot all the symptoms of her minor chest infection and she started to dither in alarm. 'Oh mercy, doctor!'

Finally Dr Ball regained enough of his breath to wheeze through the folds of his hankie, 'Have you got a cat?'

A cat, thought Sarah, well, yes, I have – two cats – but you're a doctor come to see me, not a vet. 'Oh weel, yes, there's Jackie and there's Smokey but they're both ootside just now.'

'That explains it,' gasped the doctor. 'I'm severely allergic to cats.' This information was interrupted by more sneezes, each more convulsive than the one before. As Sarah watched in consternation, the young man heaved himself from the couch and made a dive through the door and out into the open air, where he stood breathing deeply and gradually growing more calm.

Sarah hurried after him. 'Do you need a doctor, doctor?' she asked plaintively.

'No, I'm okay now,' he told her. 'Take two aspirin and rest, and if you don't feel better, could you come to the surgery?'

'Oh weel, yes.'

Dr Ball shoved his hankie back in his pocket and then started looking around as if he'd forgotten something. 'My bag. Would you be so kind . . .?'

'Oh yes,' smiled Sarah, glad at last to be useful, and she skipped back into the living room, retrieved the black bag and brought it out to Dr Ball, who took it gratefully and hurried off. His departure did not escape the notice of Jess Toft, peering through her curtains. Trying to divine what accounted for the distracted young man and the gently smiling spinster who saw him from her door kept Jess occupied for the rest of the day.

December

'Are ye seean anything?' Bowser Clett's arms were growing tired holding Cattach by the ankles.

'Yes,' shouted Cattach, his voice amplified by the wooden box he had his head in. 'I can see him all right but the beggar's no going in a straight line.'

'It's a crab,' growled Bowser. 'Fit did ee expect? Crabs go sideways.'

'He's going in a circle. If only he would go straight sideways.'

'This is a bliddy stupid idea anyway.'

Cattach ignored his helper. He was bent on finding out how fast crabs could migrate, once the creatures made up their tiny minds to proceed in one direction. To win this knowledge he had constructed a wooden box with a pane of glass in the bottom, a device that allowed him to view the bottom of the harbour without interference from reflections and wave motion.

Now he was peering at a level expanse of sand and rotten

seaware while Bowser held him over the side of the *Polaris*. In his left hand, Cattach held a stopwatch and he was trying to time the speed of a crab which they had dropped in and which was now leisurely exploring the bit of seabed where it had landed.

'I howp no chiel sees us,' cried Bowser. 'They'll think we've flipped at last and they'll be phonan for a syringe and a very strong male nurse.'

'Hold on,' cried Cattach. 'He's making a move now. Damn it – the beggar's turned back again.'

'My airms are gettan sore,' announced Bowser. 'I'm haulan ee in. In any case, there's a chiel watchan us.'

Cattach struggled back inboard and laid the box carefully on the deck. 'I told you that we have to ken how fast they move so that we move our cages at the right times. I think it would be vital to the success of any crab-ranching venture.'

'Fa's at chiel?' Bowser rolled his eyes in the direction of the quay.

Cattach put his bonnet on and looked up. A young man was standing there but he was dressed in a way neither of the experimenters had seen before. A long black coat stretched to his ankles and his hair, coloured like a peach, stuck out in spikes all around his head.

'Is that you, Mr Cattach? And yourself, Mr Clett?'

'Aye, it's us.'

'D'ye no ken me?'

Too embarrassed to admit ignorance, Cattach muttered that the light was bad. Bowser said nothing.

'I'm Mark, Mark Milton.'

Bowser and Cattach looked at each other. 'It's e minister's chiel,' mouthed Bowser. 'Fit's happened til him?'

*   *   *

'Come and see this,' shouted Alison to Dougie. The crofter came through to the kitchen to find his wife watching the midday news on the television. 'It's Amethyst Dean.'

'Fa?' asked Dougie. 'Oh, e pop singer at's bocht Brimster Hoose.'

The head of Amethyst Dean filled the small screen. She was talking cheerfully to a reporter who had obviously accosted her as she left some building in a city.

'Yes, I'm taking time out,' they heard her say. 'I need a rest. I want to think, touch base, and I've found a great place. It's peaceful, secluded, like you wouldn't believe.'

'There's a rumour it's in Scotland,' said the interviewer.

'I'm not saying where it is,' cried Amethyst, as she folded her lithe body into the back of a limousine and as a muscular minder in dark glasses glared at the camera. 'It's remote and secluded and peaceful, and I'm not telling you how to find it. Thanks, bye.'

'Well,' said Alison. 'So Brimster's still not on the map.'

'It was in e paper,' said Dougie. 'At chiels in London surely dinna read e *Groat*.'

'Maybe just as well. I don't want the paparazzi swarming up here.'

*   *   *

'So at's fit he looks like,' said Dougie, gazing with great interest at the photograph of the bog man. The face he saw was dark, wrinkled and the eyes were closed as if in sleep. On the chin stubble could be distinguished. The body, as shown in other pictures, was dressed in rough clothes resembling jute sacking.

'He's quite well-preserved,' said the Council archaeologist, on hand to tell the many visitors what he knew about the find. 'There's a lot of work to be done on him yet but the clothes indicate that he died in the early 1700s.'

'He has a peaceful expression. How did he die?' asked Alison.

'It looks as if he might have taken shelter, maybe from a blizzard, while he was crossing the hill and succumbed to exposure. But we don't know for sure. The records are poor from that time.'

Dougie turned from his scrutiny. 'So we've no idea who he was?'

'Nothing so far.'

'He reminds me o some chiel. I think he has a look o Sarah Job about him. Or Cattach.'

'Be quiet,' said Alison, giving him a dunt. 'Don't offend folk.'

'Cattach wouldna be offended. He'd be pleased. Besides if either Cattach or me looks like at in three hundred years we'll be doan weel.'

'But not Sarah Job.'

*   *   *

Miss Sarah Job was in quite a cheerful mood. For one thing, the minor chest infection brought on by too much sherry at Dougie and Alison's wedding had entirely cleared up; and for another she was looking forward to the old folks' party in the village hall, to which place she was now stepping briskly and delicately. Some other villagers were converging on the entrance, and she entered in their wake.

'Ye can sit here.' Shirley, who was on holiday from her normal duty as school dinner lady and was now in charge of roasting the turkey for the dinner, ushered the old woman to a chair.

'Thank you,' said Sarah, sitting and saying hello to everyone around her.

'Would you like a dram?' Cattach was going around with a bottle.

'Oh weel, mercy,' dithered Sarah. 'Weel, just a sensation.'

'That's what we all need,' agreed Cattach, pouring a liberal measure of a pale brown liquid. 'It's just sherry. We've fallen on hard times.'

Short Bob turned to Sarah and asked her if she had seen the photos on the wall. 'It's e mannie I found in e hill,' he explained. 'See if ye ken him.'

Shortly, Mr Milton the minister rose to his feet, welcomed everybody and said grace. Then there was a great bustle and a procession of women bearing plates of tattie soup dispensed the first course to the assembled pensioners.

'We'll be hevan music e day,' announced Short Bob between spoonfuls. 'Ian Toft is here wi his band.'

'How is his great-grandfather just now?' asked Sarah.

Short Bob wiped some stray grains of barley from his chin. 'Oh, no great. Owld Toftie's just hingan on.'

'He's a good age,' said someone.

'He's ninety-echt if he's a day,' said Bob. 'I thocht he micht make a telegram but it disna look too great ivenow. Dr Lee is goan in every day, I heard.'

Someone mentioned Dr Ball. Sarah forebore to add to the general knowledge that the poor mannie had had to run from her house because he was allergic to her cats, finished her soup, rifted very quietly into her hankie, and reached for the rest of her sherry.

'Fa achts at chiel?' said Bob suddenly, turning back from a

survey of the throng and a quick look to see if the turkey was forthcoming.

The whole table swivelled in the indicated direction. A tall, thin stranger stood beside the minister. It was not so much the long black coat, entirely encasing the man from neck to ankle, that drew their attention, but the head with its peach-coloured, spiky hair. 'He looks like a bliddy lollipop,' muttered Short Bob. As they watched, they saw Cattach approach the stranger.

'Aye, Mark,' said Cattach.

'I see you know him, Sinclair,' said the minister.

'Oh aye,' agreed Cattach. 'Would you like a refreshment, Mark?'

'No thanks, Mr Cattach,' replied the young man politely. 'I'm off for a walk before it gets dark.' And he turned and went out.

'You're lucky you knew him,' said the minister quietly. 'He goes off to the university and comes home in that disguise. His mother and I are no too happy about the hair and metal jewellery, but he has to find his own way.'

'It's just a phase he's going through,' said Cattach. 'It's a fashion.'

'I suppose you're right. But I'm thinking of asking him to dye his hair black before he comes to the kirk again.'

The rest of the dinner passed without incident except for a minor kerfuffle when Short Bob got into difficulty with a caramel and at once had to remove both sets of dentures to deal with it.

January

For three whole days over the New Year a hush lay over Brimster. In the streets of the village very little traffic was seen to move. Occasionally a pedestrian ventured out for a walk and could be seen, for example, being dragged along by a dog from one gatepost to the next, or wandering in the direction of the harbour just for 'a turn' to breathe fresh air or burn off some of the excess consumption in which everyone had indulged. There were so few people to be seen that Jess Toft even abandoned for a while watching from her window.

Beyond the village, out among the crofts and farms, there were more signs of life as, to a great extent, work there had to go on. The animals had to be fed, maybe a little later in the day than usual, but still fed. Dougie came in from giving hay to his sheep to find Short Bob's tractor parked beside the house and the old crofter himself in the kitchen, sitting with a mug of coffee, newsing with Alison. They wished each other a good New Year, and Bob fumbled through the many layers of ganseys he wore to withdraw from some hidden pocket a bottle of whisky.

'It was very quiet,' said Bob.

Not many would have struggled as far as Whin City to first-foot Bob. Indeed, not many had come by Dougie's and Alison's croft, but for once they had been glad of a tranquil Hogmanay.

'Here's fun,' said Dougie, tossing back a dram.

'Here's til it,' echoed Bob. 'It's no muckle but it's all at's for it. If I canna scratch a living I can still scratch my backside. Fan's e bairn due?'

'Oh, the bairn?' said Alison. 'Not until March.'

'E middle e lambing,' nodded Bob.

Later, Dougie told Alison that he hadn't meant to be rude, it was just his way of reckoning time.

*   *   *

Cattach meandered down the road to the shore, his bonnet firmly pulled down over his forehead and his hands deep in his pockets. He was musing over the advantages of making homebrew and possibly searching on the internet for information, now that he had his computer up and running and was getting to grips with double clicks, websites and email. He paused for a moment in his reverie and looked out over the grey sea. At the foot of the brae lay the harbour, and all the boats.

'Hello, Mr Cattach.'

The voice belonged to a young man, strangely dressed in a

long black coat and with peach-coloured hair, sitting in the lee of a shed.

'Aye, Mark, it's yoursel,' said Cattach. 'Sore head e day?'

'No much chance o that in the manse.'

'I've seen Mr Milton take a drammie,' said Cattach, wandering over to sit down beside him. 'As far as I can mind, e Lord turned watter intil wine at e feast at Cana. He widna hev done at if he didna want ee til hev a drammie. Now and again, of course.'

Mark laughed. 'Dad's fond o talking wi you. He says you have an original mind.'

'Did he say at? Weel, maybe,' mused Cattach. 'May I ask you a personal question?'

'Aye, sure.'

'I noticed you have a ring in your ear, and a stud in your nose. Does it signify anything?'

'No really. Just fancied it. Oh, I know what you're thinking. My faither being e minister, it seems a bit extreme. He's pretty cool aboot it, actually. He sees it as some kind o spirituality.'

'I thocht e stud in your tongue wid be a bit o a humbowg eating fried herring. Ye ken, the bones and all.'

'I'm vegetarian, but I admit celery can be a problem. I usually take it out when I eat.'

'I had a tattoo done once,' said Cattach. 'In the navy. I was in the Faroes. Have you ever thocht about Atlantis?'

*　　*　　*

Magnus Stroup, councillor, driving instructor and part-time agricultural salesman, stirred from his house and went along the street to buy a newspaper and a packet of five Hamlet cigars from Jean in the shop.

'A good New Year to you,' said Magnus.

'Gled til see e back o id,' said Jean, punching the till and stuffing in Magnus's payment.

'I dare say.' Magnus was in too benign a mood to care about Jean's girning and flicked open the paper to view the headlines. 'What's happening in the world now, I wonder.'

'Naethin but floods, disasters and bad news,' affirmed Jean.

Magnus sometimes wondered if Jean counted herself among his supporters. He had been councillor for a long time now, an independent, holding himself free from the disciplines of any party so that he could serve his electors according to principle and conscience. Thanks to his efforts, a faulty street lamp had been repaired, the road to the harbour had been tarred, and a new picnic site and public convenience, with up-to-date disabled facilities, was planned to attract tourists to the harbour. Of course, as no one had stood against him for years, it didn't matter whether Jean voted for him or not.

'Aye, maybe it does seem that way,' he agreed benignly, as he scanned the paper. 'You know, sometimes I don't know about these tabloids. They reduce everything to a very low level of argument.'

Jean frowned. Was he going to stand there the whole day? Then, Magnus shut his mouth, folded the paper hastily, and hurried out to the street, throwing the words 'Cheerio, then' over his shoulder like an afterthought. Jean's frown deepened. Odd, one minute he looks as if he's here for the day, the next he's off as if he's taken a dose of syrup of figs. After years of running the post office and the shop, Jean had a keen sense for detecting something new. She didn't like change but she could feel it coming on before anyone else and occasionally at an astonishing distance. Nothing went off her. If clash could be said to have a smell, then Jean was one of the rare beings who had the nostrils to sniff it. Magnus's hasty departure from the shop smelled very strongly of something brewing. So, as Magnus was a bit full of himself and often tedious, she began to leaf through another copy of the paper he had bought. She had reached the middle pages and had so far found nothing when the bell tinkled above the front door and Miss Sarah Job edged timidly in.

As Sarah went up and down the aisles and put things in her basket, Jean folded the paper carefully, smoothed it with her hands and slid it back into the pile for sale.

'Any word o Owld Toftie?' asked Jean.

'He's rallied a bit,' said Sarah. 'I was speaking til Jess. But they're ready for e worst, and as long's he's comfortable.'

'Aye, he's a good age, richt enough.'

'Elsie was in.'

Jean paused over the till. 'Oh weel, he must be gettan near e bottom e brae, in at case.'

'Oh weel,' murmured Sarah.

Both of them knew, of course, that Jess Toft and Elsie Ham, sisters, did not normally have much to say to each other. They also knew that Owld Toftie, who had been round the world several times as a merchant seaman in his day, was expected to leave a fair penny or two behind him.

'They're both widows,' said Sarah.

Jean said nothing in response to this unnecessary remark.

'He'll likely leave something til both families,' said Sarah.

'Weel, it micht make sense til share it atween e Tofts and e Hams,' whispered Jean, leaning towards Sarah across the counter, a move that made Sarah instinctively go back a step. 'Both big families, mind, but Owld Toftie was never very keen on Elsie merryan a Ham.'

The tinkling of the bell interrupted their discussion. Jean heaved herself upright. Sarah coughed politely and began to rummage in her purse. 'Mr Milton, it's yourself,' announced Jean, as the minister came forward to the counter.

The minister collected his newspaper, told the two women he was off to town to see Mark away on the train, and went out again.

'Mark's doing very well,' whispered Sarah.

Jean frowned. 'He'd do better til wash at dye oot o his hair. I dinna ken fit they do at at universities.'

'Talkan aboot universities, I hear at Fiona and Catriona Stroup are doan weel. Clever lassies,' said Sarah.

'Must hev got e brains fae their mither's side,' was Jean's only comment, thinking about their father's visit earlier.

*   *   *

Dreep and Pogo were sitting in the public bar of the Brimster Arms, empty pint glasses and empty crisp packets before them. The Mansons' old Labrador came up and sniffed at the packets, looked at the two young men and turned away with a mournful look and a sad wag of his tail.

'Dowg's gettan owld,' observed Pogo.

'Aye,' said Dreep. 'Ee for anither?'

'No, I'm cleaned oot. Canna afford even anither bag o crisps.'

'Same here. I've a driving lesson wi Magnus at e end e week. Micht hev til cancel it. I've nothing til pay him wi. I still think we should hev got a reward for findan at feet in e bin.'

'I've an idea,' said Pogo with an energy that annoyed Dreep.

'Fit?'

'Rabbits.'

'Rabbits? They dinna give driving lessons.'

'Sell them. Catch them and sell them til a butcher. Wi iss BSE, fowk can eat rabbits.'

'Bliddy daft.'

'Hev ee ever heard o mad rabbit disease? It's good grub. Ma faither used til catch them wi snares and sell them til butchers. They're free for e taking.'

Pogo grew more convinced of the brilliance of his own idea the more he talked about it, and his enthusiasm finally got through to his pal, who asked suspiciously, 'How do we do it?'

'Snares. We can set snares at nicht and go back in e mornane. We hev til gut them and clean them but I can ask ma mither til do at. If she'll no do it – come til think o it, we'd better do it wirsels efter all – but it's no hard.'

'Far will we get them?'

'E hill. E hill's fill o rabbits, especially up aboot Whin City and ower aboothan wi Brimster Hoose.'

'No, I mean, far will we get snares?'

Pogo beamed. 'I've got a lot o them in e shed at e hoose. Ma faither's. They just need a bit o a dustane. Come on, I'll show ee.'

*   *   *

Dreep was not happy. It was cold and it would soon be dark, and he and Pogo were out in the hill a long way from warm rooms, bars and anything else that could be associated with bodily comfort. 'I dinna think iss is a good idea,' he said.

'It's just a scouting trip,' shouted Pogo, hurrying on up the track. 'We'll no be long. At least it's dry.' At that moment, he splashed through a pool of peaty water.

'Dinna go so fast, then.' They fanged up over a ridge of ground, into the teeth of the wind, and Dreep pulled his woolly hat tighter over his lugs and stumbled on.

After more purgatory, Pogo stopped and crouched down.

'Hev ye hurt yoursel?' asked Dreep.

'Shut up. See.'

Dreep looked but did not see. 'Fit is it?'

'Rabbits. Howld your tongue.'

At last, Dreep distinguished grey ghosts slipping past a whin bush and disappearing into the dark bowels of the earth. 'Right,' said Pogo. 'We can set e snares here.'

Dreep hoped that they could then turn for home but his expectation had only a short life. 'I've still got half a dozen,' announced Pogo. 'We'll find anither spot.' And the hunters carried on down the boggy, stony track as the darkness deepened around them. They had reached a slightly better road and clumps of whins when they heard a whup-whup noise.

'Fitna beastie's at?' cried Dreep in alarm.

'At's no a beastie,' said Pogo. 'Look. It's a helicopter.'

True enough. High above them a cluster of lights beat across the sky but soon, to their great interest, the cluster seemed to slow and then descend.

'Are ye sure it's a helicopter?' murmured Dreep. 'Fowk hev seen UFOs up here, ee ken.'

'At wis Shirley's man and he had a fill at e time. It's a helicopter richt enough.' Pogo paused. 'Weel, it must be a helicopter. Ye dinna believe in all at rubbish aboot Martians, do ee?'

'Oh no,' said Dreep hastily.

The lights had disappeared and the whup-whup sound had died away. It seemed suddenly very dark. They drew their anoraks about them and followed the hill road for a bit, until they came to a thick copse of whins and broom. 'There micht be something here,' whispered Pogo confidently, and he dropped to his hands and knees and began to feel his way around the edge of the spiky bushes.

'I canna see far ee are,' hissed Dreep.

'Just bide ere, then.'

Dreep thought that it would be better not to stand alone too long in the dark and edged forward. 'Hev ee got e torch?' No answer came from Pogo. Dreep increased his pace, a move that only brought him sooner into hard contact with the whins. He swore loudly as the needles pierced his jeans and then his knees.

'Stay where you are!'

The voice was loud, very close and not Pogo's, and was accompanied by a blinding beam of white light. Dreep froze, dazzled, his eyes wide, his mouth wider. But only for a split second before he let out a howl, tore himself loose from the whins and sprinted away down the road.

*   *   *

Sinclair Cattach could hardly open his door fast enough to admit the bustling figure of Bowser Clett. 'I was just coming round,' said Cattach, 'to work on the crab cage. What's your hurry.'

'Never heed crabs,' cried Bowser. 'Hev ee seen iss?' He brandished a copy of a newspaper and, in his excitement, forgot the ferocious nature of Cattach's cat and shoved it from the table. With a loud growl, the beast scuttled off to the kitchen. Bowser opened the paper and pointed to the page spread before him.

Cattach peered down at it.

'Ere,' cried Bowser, stabbing a photograph.

The picture showed a number of faces, happy faces, mostly female though, on closer inspection, the moustached visage of a man was plainly among them. The man's eyes were half-closed and the plump cheeks conveyed an expression of contentment such as might be seen on a Santa half-seas over.

'Well, now,' breathed Cattach. 'I think I know that man.'

'Ee ken him all richt. We all ken him. At's wir councillor.'

Cattach chuckled. 'Fit's Magnus been up til?' He read aloud the caption: 'Highland councillor caught in red-light area junket.'

'I could hardly get intil e shop,' said Bowser. 'There wis a crowd at e counter fechtan for copies o e paper, and Jean wis ringan e till til e keys were reid-hot.'

Cattach read on. The gist was that, after a fact-finding mission to the European Parliament, some Highland councillors had

found their way into the streets of Amsterdam where they had obviously been celebrating a successful tour. Among them had been Brimster's own representative, Magnus Stroup.

'Well, it's just like Magnus to have been doing his bit for international relations,' observed Cattach. 'Hey, at ane wasna born yesterday. See e wrinkles roond her eyes.'

'Ee can just aboot see e wrinkles roond everything she's got,' said Bowser. 'I wonder how Magnus will explain iss on his expenses.'

*   *   *

'Come on, Annabella. Ye're thrawn e day.' Dougie's complaint failed to persuade the goat to budge from the tuft of grass she was chewing at the roadside. He gave up pulling on the tether and waited. Annabella raised her head, gave him a mysterious look with her yellow eye and trotted for a few yards. 'Ach, ee'll do here,' he said, and drove the backie into the turf with the heel of his boot. 'Ee can eat some o that grass for a change.'

Alison drove out from the house in the van and, as she drew level with her husband, stopped to let him in to the passenger seat. Bess the collie squeezed to one side to give him some room. They drove down the road towards the village. This was Alison's idea, a break from her own kitchen to have a bar lunch in the Brimster Arms.

'I'm really hungry,' she said. 'I hope there's something good and fatty on the menu. Oh I know, I should mind my diet but, once in a while, it'll no do harm.'

'I widna think so,' agreed Dougie.

Alison's swollen, pregnant middle almost touched the steering wheel.

As they drove on, they met two men coming up the road on foot, two men they recognised as Pogo and Dreep. Alison slowed the van and Dougie wound down the window. 'Fit ee on e day?'

'Hev ee rabbits?' asked Pogo, talking without removing his roll-up from his lips. Dougie said that there were some at the end of his land and they could set their snares there, if they wanted.

'We got two last nicht,' said Pogo. 'Could've had more if we hadna been chased off.'

'Chased off?'

Dreep bent his head to the window and explained how a man from Brimster House had told them they were trespassing. Pogo laughed: 'Dreep thocht he was a Martian come til kidnap him.'

'I did not,' protested his companion. 'Dougie, he said at it was private property around Brimster Hoose now and we had no richt til be ere. Is at richt?'

'I dinna ken,' said the crofter. 'Fit harm were ee doan in any case? Except til e rabbits, I suppose.'

'Maybe Amethyst Dean's minders thought you were paparazzi,' said Alison. 'Spying on her in her retreat.'

'We werena papa . . . papa-anything,' complained Dreep. 'It's no richt. Bliddy pop star incomers.'

With that, the rabbit hunters continued on their way. Alison and Dougie drove across the burn and up the slight brae into the centre of the village. They stopped outside the Brimster Arms. While Alison went into the bar, Dougie nipped across the road to the shop to get some messages. As he went through the door and as the bell clattered above his head, a woman rushed out past him without so much as a word, forcing him to stand back against the shop freezer.

'Peggy's in a hurry e day,' he observed.

This remark was met with silence. Jean stood behind the till with what could have been a smile on her face. Miss Sarah Job and Elsie Ham wore equally inscrutable expressions.

*　　*　　*

Peggy Stroup knew that the whole village would be watching her now and had decided that the only thing to do was to act as if nothing were amiss. But this decision of the brain had not influenced her feet which, still guided by instinct, knew that she had to hurry. So, she stepped briskly away from the shop and strode along the pavement, past the houses, the hotel, the school, and the hall, all the way towards the bungalow with the dormer windows where she lived.

As she came close to home, she heard voices calling. She slowed and moved cautiously along the privet hedge that fringed the large garden. She felt alone. Her daughters, Fiona and Catriona, were both away at university and doing well, and probably did not yet know what had happened. She would have to phone them soon to let them know that a photograph of their father in an Amsterdam brothel had just been published in a newspaper.

When she reached the end of the hedge and had a clear view of her front door, she stopped in shock. A man was on the patio, on his knees, and he appeared to be shouting loudly at the door. Then she saw that this man, who had dark hair and thick glasses, was holding the letterbox open with his fingers.

'Magnus, it's me, Alecker Munro,' the man was shouting. 'You'll have to speak to me. Give me your side of the story.'

'Go away,' came a faint roar from inside the house, a roar that Peggy recognised as belonging to her husband. 'Go away. I'm not talking til the press.'

'Magnus,' continued Alecker. 'Magnus, it is you in that photo. Do you deny it's yourself? If you dinna give me your side of the story, they'll make it up.'

Peggy stood rooted to the pavement. At first she didn't know what to do. The journalist was in plain view, now on his hunkers on the doormat, his fingers holding open the flap of the letterbox. On the other side, she could imagine her husband, kneeling on the expensive carpet, blue with gold flecks, that they had laid only a month ago. Shame burned in her face but she was made of pretty stout stuff and refused to look round to see if Brimster was watching. The situation demanded urgent action. Alecker had to be silenced. She could deal with her errant husband in her own good time. Quickly she ran up the pavement.

'Look, Magnus, it's better that you talk to me before the others . . .' Alecker was saying when Peggy's right foot caught him with some force in the rear end. In the same adroit move, Peggy's right hand turned the doorknob and pushed the door open. It flashed through her mind that Magnus the gowk had neglected to lock it but, for once, she forgave him, particularly as her sudden assault cracked the door against her husband's head on the other side.

Magnus fell back, clutching his brow, Alecker fell in and sprawled on the new, expensive, gold-flecked, blue carpet and Peggy shoved them both aside and slammed the door shut behind her. She clicked the sneck on the lock and turned to survey the body count.

'My heid!' moaned Magnus. Alecker was rubbing his hips and scrabbling for his glasses.

'What a pair!' declared Peggy. 'Get up, the both o ye. Alecker Munro, ye've got a nerve coming here after scandal, when I could tell a good story or two about your mither. And, as for ye, Magnus, take your hands away fae your heid and shut up before I give ye a slap.'

The councillor and the journalist could think of nothing to say.

'Go til e kitchen, both o ye, and sit doon,' said Peggy. As they struggled to their feet, she made a quick recce through the curtains of the road outside and, to her satisfaction, saw nothing.

'I can explain everything, darling . . .' began Magnus.

'Howld your tongue. Dinna darling me.'

'Mrs Stroup . . . eh, Peggy . . . listen,' Alecker spoke up. 'I know you're upset but it's better Magnus gives me the full story.'

'Full story. So ye can print it and bring further shame on us. Ye've always done it. What did you say when my husband focht hard til get a new public lavatory and picnic site? "Magnus Stroup goes to the wall." What d'ye call at?'

Alecker girned. 'It was just a figure of speech. But this is serious. The guys from the nationals are on their way here. You'll be doorstepped. It's a good story.'

'I can explain . . . I was set up,' cried Magnus.

The journalist and the enraged wife both ignored him. Peggy stared at Alecker and immediately realised he was right. 'D'ye guarantee til write the truth?'

'Absolutely,' said Alecker quickly. 'Exclusive rights.'

She was taking in what that might mean when the doorbell rang.

'Stay here,' commanded Peggy. She went through to the hall and saw through the frosted glass of the door the shadow of someone on the front step. The bell rang again. At the same time the telephone bleeped. She pulled the socket from the wall and ran up the stairs to the bedroom, from where she had a clear view of the garden. Two cars were now parked in front of the house and, as she watched, a third drew up. A small knot of men and women, all strangers, and some bearing large cameras, had gathered at the gate.

She went quickly back to the kitchen, pulled the curtains and whirled to face Alecker. 'All right,' she said. 'They're here. What's your plan, and it better be a good one.'

*   *   *

Dougie and Alison were finishing their bar lunch in the Brimster Arms when Alecker burst in. Apart from Sinclair Cattach perched on a stool and drinking a pint, the bar was empty. Alecker adjusted his jacket and his glasses, and sat down beside the crofter.

'Dougie,' he hissed. 'I need a hand. Is that your van ootside, wi the dog in it?' He didn't wait for an answer and hurriedly went on. 'You know about Magnus's photo. Well, now he's besieged by the big paper boys fae the south. He's needs you.'

'Haud on a minute,' said Dougie. 'I dinna ken fit ye're on aboot. Fit's Magnus's photo got til do wi me?'

'If our councillor wants to enjoy himself in a Dutch bordello, that's his business,' said Alison.

'No, no,' said Alecker. 'This is something else. I want to get Magnus and Peggy away without being followed.'

'Ye've got a car o your ain.'

'The paparazzi know me. Your van is anonymous.'

Suddenly Cattach was standing beside the table. 'I couldna help owerhearing,' he said slowly. 'Now this getaway business you're talking o, this would be smuggling Magnus fae under the noses o ootsiders, am I right?'

'Bang on,' cried Alecker with excitement.

'Then I'm thinking your plan isna foolproof,' said Cattach. He paused and added softly, 'You need a diversion.'

*   *   *

The foosim van drove slowly past the throng outside the Stroup residence. And it was quite a throng. About a dozen men and women, some with cameras, others with notebooks and microphones, milled about on the pavement and up the path to the front door. One man had erected a stepladder and was standing on it for a better view.

'I know some of them,' whispered Alecker, keeping his head low between the two front seats. 'See that guy in the blue anorak. He's Aberdeen. And that blonde, she's Glasgow. Magnus could be front-page news.'

'I don't think Magnus wants to be front-page anything,' said Alison, smiling and waving as reporters moved aside to avoid the van.

'It's his own fault,' muttered Dougie. 'Fancy gettan himsel

catched wi his trousers doon. In a manner o speakan. Far's Cattach and his diversion?'

No sooner had his name been mentioned than Cattach's gangly frame appeared in the rear-view mirror. The old fellow was ambling down the road towards the paparazzi.

'Okay, good,' said Alecker. 'Go on a bit, and turn doon the lane that swings back behind Magnus's.'

As the van passed on, Cattach reached his target.

'Well, well, well,' he said loudly, and then repeated it for the satisfaction of seeing how the news-hungry hacks all turned to look at him. 'This is a bit of excitement for Brimster, I must say. Is it a sale o work?'

*　　*　　*

Dougie edged the van along the narrow lane. A broken flag dyke and a wire fence stood between them and a small park. Beyond the park a short distance rose the concrete wall around the Stroup's back green.

'Peggy should be watching.' Alecker was growing very pleased with the way the plan was working out and he grinned broadly when he saw the curtain on the kitchen window flick. Seconds later, the back door opened and Magnus Stroup scuttled out, closely followed by his wife. They scurried through a little gate and across the grass to the fence. Here progress was impeded for a few moments by Magnus's lack of athletic ability but a heave from Peggy got him through. Alecker already had the back door of the van open, and helped them in, while the twanging of barbed wire still echoed up the lane.

'What now?' asked Dougie.

'Anywhere,' said Alecker.

'Home?' said Alison to her husband.

'I'm sorry til trouble ye like this, Dougie.' Magnus had found his politician's voice again and would have said more, if Peggy had not hit him and pointed to the gash the barbed wire had torn in his trousers.

'Just sit ticht and keep quiet,' said Dougie. 'We'll hev til take iss canny.'

The lane led them gradually back towards the main road. From the junction they could see the press outside the bungalow and among them Cattach.

'So, ye see,' Cattach was saying, 'I think grey hair does grow faster than normal hair. I've come to this conclusion after many years' thocht, after five years in the Royal Navy, umpteen years at the seine-net fishing, and even longer at self-study o marine biology, archaeology and history. Some o ye might question my lack o academic qualifications but I believe this is a free country and a man should be able til speak his mind . . .'

'Are you a relative of Councillor Stroup?' shouted someone.

'We're all one here,' replied Cattach in a scriptural tone.

'How does the village feel about the behaviour of its councillor?' Camera lenses swung towards Cattach.

'As I said, it's a free country, and if Magnus wants til escape the stresses and cares o office by spending some leisure time in a popular tourist attraction that's fine by me.'

'It was a brothel,' declared the Glaswegian blonde.

'Allegedly,' nodded Cattach, trying not to show he was enjoying himself but desperately thinking of things to say.

'So, it's okay to go to a brothel,' came another reporter.

'People who live in glass houses should not cast the first stone,' answered Cattach.

'Right on, old timer,' laughed the Aberdonian in the anorak.

'So, brothels are okay,' cried a young man in a stylish suit.

'That's typical of the sexist crap your paper prints,' objected the blonde.

'What's your paper, then? The kirk monthly?'

The cameraman on the stepladder had forgotten the Stroups' curtains and was focusing on his colleagues. Cattach turned to present his best side and tried to look stern and outraged.

'Now that you've come all this way,' he began, 'I can take iss opportunity til point oot a few o the many items o interest in this village. You can see the school down there, and the new hall, and the Brimster Arms where delicious, fresh bar meals are to be had daily . . . and then there's the shop . . .'

*   *   *

Magnus had a hard time trying to explain that he had been the victim of circumstance. Alison was almost feeling sorry for him, the picture of shame and dejection he made, sitting at the end of her kitchen table, his hands clutching a mug of coffee with a slug of rum in it. Alecker was busily recording what the councillor had to say. Dougie seemed more amused than anything else. Peggy, Magnus's wife, was everything but amused.

'Look at ee,' she was railing. 'What a sicht! A man o your years and maturity, the faither o two dochters at the university, a councillor for goodness knows how long, a respected member o this community – and look at ee!'

Dougie thought 'respected member' was laying it on a bit but held his tongue.

'It wasna my fault,' pleaded the councillor, his moustache wriggling on his lip like a mouse trying to escape. 'I was set up. It was at councillors fae Belgium and Spain, they took me wi them.'

'Ee could've stopped in e hotel and said no,' growled Peggy.

'I thocht I was being sociable and I felt the honour o my country was at stake.' The sound of the words seemed to remind Magnus of his heritage and his dignity, and he straightened in his chair. 'Besides I didna do anything.'

'At doesna surprise me,' said Peggy bitterly.

'I mean, we had a few drinks and there were some funny fags, and I canna mind e rest. I mean I'm sure I didna do anything. Honest.'

*   *   *

That Magnus may have failed to avail himself of all that was on offer in an Amsterdam house of pleasure would have come as disappointing news to at least three members of the community he claimed to represent. Pogo and Dreep had cut out the notorious photograph of the self-martyred councillor and had stuck it up in the cab of the scaffie lorry with the words WUR HERO felt-tipped across it in sprawling capitals.

'I wonder fit it's lek in one o at places,' said Pogo. 'D'ye think it's dear?'

'See at owld wifie on Magnus's lap,' mused Dreep. 'He didna go wi her, did he? If I was him I'd take e ither one. She looks as if she hasna reached her sell-by date.'

Lang Tam frowned. 'I'm no too keen on Magnus's photo up ere. It doesna seem richt at we, council employees, should be drivan aroond e whole day wi a councillor watchan us.'

'No need til worry,' cried Pogo. 'He's got his een shut in e photo anyway. He canna see us.'

Dreep felt the conversation was taking a surreal turn and changed the subject by asking 'Far are we goan?'

'Brimster House,' announced Lang Tam, slowing and turning the lorry in at a gate they were not accustomed to enter. 'Now at it's occupied again, it's been added til e round. Here we are, boys, scaffies til e rich and famous, rubbish collectors til e celebrities. Mind, Dreep, no lookan in e wheelie bins.'

Amethyst Dean, pop idol, was now the owner of Brimster House, although so far she had not been seen in the village and the only indication of her movements had been the occasional throb of a helicopter.

There was only one bin for the men to attend to. Dreep did of course have a quick glance inside while Lang Tam turned the lorry but the survey didn't tell him much, only that Amethyst Dean put out her garbage in a black plastic bag like everyone else.

'Hey, see iss,' cried Pogo. He pointed to a wooden sign hammered into the roadside on a stake. The sign read 'Private – No Admittance'.

Dreep scowled and dropped shut the lid of the bin. 'I dinna like at kind o thing, d'ye?'

The lorry was bleeping and blinking as Lang Tam backed towards them. Fresh in the minds of Pogo and Dreep was the night they had been chased from the grounds of the House when they had only been after some rabbits. Pogo bent, pulled the sign from the ground and tossed it into the back of the lorry.

*　　*　　*

'It looks no bad,' said Cattach, standing back and admiring his handiwork. 'I dare say the design will need a few refinements but we'll only find at oot by experiment.'

'I dinna see how we're goan til get it oot e door,' said Bowser. 'It looks awful big.'

'Six feet by six feet, and two feet deep. It'll go through e door on its end. I've measured it. We should have built it ootside.'

'No way,' declared Bowser. He didn't want anyone to know that he had allowed himself to be talked into the venture of crab-ranching. 'We'll wait til it's dark and carry it aboard e boat. E tide's richt for an early start next week.'

The large cage they had made still needed stones to weight it and keep it on the seabed, but these could be added later.

'How early?' asked Cattach.

'Three o'clock,' said Bowser.

'At's e middle e nicht.'

'I ken but I'm takan no chance at Wildy Ham will see us.'

March

The news that Owld Toftie had finally passed away, at the age of ninety-eight, spread quickly around Brimster, and stirred in its wake speculation over what he might have left to his heirs – and who those heirs might be.

'I dinna believe he was at weel off,' said John Campbell. 'He lived on an oily rag.'

'Oh weel,' replied Miss Sarah Job, failing to see that John was winding her up when he said this to her in the shop, 'He went around the world a lot o times and came back a rich man, they say.'

'It's always e rich at live in a funny way,' declared Jean behind the counter, in a show of solidarity with Sarah that momentarily startled the old spinster. 'Just ee wait and see.'

Brimster did wait and what Brimster was to see kept the place amused for quite a while. In the meantime, Dougie and Alison had more pressing business. The first of their two cows decided to give birth to her calf at four o'clock in the morning.

'Ye could have picked a better time, Chrissie,' growled Dougie to the animal, as he stood in the byre and watched Chrissie lick and nuzzle her newly arrived offspring.

'He looks healthy enough,' said Alison, sitting down on the feedbox. 'In fact, he looks better than I feel right now.'

'Ye're no . . .?'

'No, still two or three weeks to go,' Alison sighed. 'Aye, you can look, Chrissie. Now I know how you felt.'

It had been some pull to bring the calf into the world but at least they hadn't had to summon the vet. She could look in later to confirm that all was well.

'What a spring for youngsters,' said Dougie, sitting on the box beside his wife. 'Chrissie done, Snowdrop til come, e sheep til lamb, and yoursel. If they are all like iss nicht, at'll be fine.'

*   *   *

The day of Owld Toftie's funeral arrived. Sinclair Cattach and
Bowser Clett took their places in the long trail of dark-clad figures
following the hearse to the cemetery. Cattach had on a rather
smart trilby. Bowser wore the bowler hat he always used for last
rites.

'It looks as if e whole clan is here,' said Cattach softly.

'They're all lookan for fit they can get,' muttered Bowser.

Cattach glanced at his companion. Bowser's wife, Isobel, was
a distant cousin of the Tofts but before Cattach's mind raced away
on its own conclusion Bowser added, '. . . but we're no expectan
nor seekan anything. Toftie was a fine mannie in his way . . .'
Other men in the cortège spoke a greeting to the fisherman as
they passed, and Bowser paused until they were out of earshot
before resuming his commentary. '. . . A fine mannie, and there's
more than one bottle at we killed off atween us.'

'I've heard he kept a tin box below his bed, and kept e key on
a string around his neck at all times,' said Cattach.

'I dinna ken aboot no box,' replied Bowser hastily, 'and on e last time I saw him he had naethane roond his neck but a tidemark.'

The hearse stopped at the cemetery gate, and the procession paused.

'He's got a good turn oot,' commented Cattach.

'Look at them all.' Bowser's tone was low. 'Ere's Jess Toft and Elsie Ham, e two dochters. Fit are they doan here? Walkan side by side, at hevna spoken one til e ither til their owld faither weighed his anchor.'

The Tofts – Jess, her son Ian, and her daughters Nellie and Greta – and the Hams, led by Elsie, her daughter Ina, and her sons Wildy and Harry – Harry had flown north for the occasion and was better known as Horace because he wore thick glasses like Horace Broon – led the mourners to the graveside where Mr Milton, the minister, waited to officiate.

The threatening rain kept off and the wind died away until the whisper of the surf on the shore could be heard. As the minister went through the rites, Cattach thought the old seaman would have liked that, the faint farewell of the waves. The service came to an end and, with a donning of headgear and a burst of low conversation, the crowd turned to disperse.

Amid the slow ebb of mourners, Cattach was suddenly surprised to see Jess Toft rush through the cemetery gate, gesturing to Nellie and Greta to keep close on her tail. Then he saw that Elsie Ham and her entourage were likewise hurrying towards the waiting cars with grim faces. There was almost a knocking aside of disinterested parties and, with a chorus of slamming doors and revving engines, the two cars set off at some lick back towards the village.

From her front window, Sarah Job saw the Tofts arrive first, only seconds before the Hams, at the house across the street. Jess Toft was out and up the path, fumbling in her handbag as she went, but Elsie was not far behind and, by putting on an extra spurt, reached the front door just as her sister disappeared inside. They were closely followed by Horace Ham. Sarah was so overcome by this strange, hurried procession that she began to describe it to her cats: 'There's Wildy now. That's Elsie's son, and that's her daughter, Ina. They are no going in. That's them standing on the pavement. Well now, Wildy looks a wee bit embarrassed, is that no strange, Smokey?'

Smokey looked with incomprehension at his mistress, as Sarah went on: 'There's Nellie now and Greta – oh they're both for going in, and Nellie has pushed past Wildy Ham. Wildy is saying something. I wish I had left the window open. Oh weel, it might not have been very nice. Wait, though, here's Ian Toft – he's awful like his grandfather – oh he's speaking til Wildy. They're both shaking their heads, Smokey.'

If Sarah had been able to see through the house walls she would have discovered Elsie and Jess jammed in the doorway into Owld Toftie's bedroom. Both were on the heavy side and, as neither would give way to the other, they had become stuck between the jambs. The sisters found themselves locked against each other, like two great, black-clad icebergs, their faces inches apart.

'He left it til me,' gasped Jess.

'It's mine,' peched Elsie. 'I was born first.'

'Ye never came near him for many a day.'

'Some o us . . . Oooh!'

Horace Ham, coming close behind, saw that action was required, and he pushed hard against his mother. But he didn't have the strength and failed to budge them, and had to retreat to search for his glasses when his mother's elbow knocked them from his nose. Greta, Ina and Nellie had a go but their combined efforts failed to shift the sisters.

Wildy Ham and Ian Toft then appeared and stopped in amazement at the sight of the scrum. 'Mither!' they both cried together, although addressing two different women. 'Push, Wildy,' shouted Elsie and Ina. 'Push, Ian,' wheezed Jess, Greta and Nellie. But Ian and Wildy looked at each other and said with one voice, 'We should leave them both together.'

Horace found his wits with his glasses and spoke up: 'Come on, let's get iss ower wi.'

The three men rushed their jammed mothers and, with a great riving and screaming, all five burst like an exploding cork through the door into the bedroom, with the other three women tumbling after them. Jess recovered first and rushed to the side of the bed but Elsie wasn't far behind and scrambled to the other side. Both reached in together, both laid their grip on an end of the iron-bound box that for years had sat under the springs, slowly rusting and gathering stoor, and both heaved to no effect.

'Can we no open it together?' shouted Wildy.

His mother, his auntie, his cousins and his sister looked at him as if he had announced something so original that none could take it in at once.

Wildy turned to his cousin, Ian, and said, 'Come on, we'll open e bliddy box and at'll be e end o iss carry-on.'

They dragged the box out on to the carpet and got down on their knees around it. Horace polished his glasses for a better view, while the women jostled for a good position.

'Key!' demanded Wildy.

The old man had entrusted the key to a solicitor and this solicitor had passed the key, as per instruction, to Jess at the funeral. She reluctantly held it out towards her nephew. It was polished and shiny. Wildy slid the key into the lock. It turned stiffly, but it turned and Wildy felt the lock give way.

'Ready?' he asked, looking around at his relatives.

'Open it,' whispered his mother, Elsie.

Wildy began reverently to lift the lid and all their eyes widened at the prospect of seeing the contents they had been thirsting to know for many a day. Owld Toftie had sailed around the world several times in the merchant navy – there was hardly a port or a bar between Valparaiso and Saint Petersburg that hadn't known his tread – and every time he had come home rumours had fluttered in his wake like a flock of gulls. He had traded in diamonds, he had run guns in the Middle East, he had stumbled on El Dorado, he had fathered an Amazon tribe that still worshipped his likeness, he had picked up a nugget of gold on a Canadian beach. Now all was about to be revealed to his daughters and his grandchildren.

'Nothing,' breathed Wildy. 'Bugger all. E owld chiel had us on a leash for nothing.'

'Ye've been in iss box already, ya limmer,' shouted Elsie to her sister.

'No, I wisna,' cried Jess. 'I widna steal e key fae ma faither. Are ee sure ye didna?'

'Are ee callan me a thief?' challenged Elsie.

'Shut up, the both o ye,' shouted Horace, leaning in for a closer inspection of the box. He began to tap with his knuckles. Two little taps at intervals around the edge of the bottom that beat out a regular rhythm like a soft drum. Their hearts all fell into the same rhythm until Ian broke the spell: 'Doesna sound hollow til me. I'm a musician. Ye can tell.'

Horace continued to tap his knuckles around the bottom of the box, while the relatives watched, hardly daring to breathe. 'There's nothing there,' said Ian Toft.

'Fit would he keep an empty box below the bed for?' cried his aunt, Greta Leavad.

'Sentimental reasons,' suggested her nephew. 'Memories.'

'Wait!' Horace's cry made them all freeze. Peering over his thick glasses, Horace scanned the row of faces around him and tapped again. 'That bit sounds hollow,' he whispered.

They crowded in for a closer look and almost tumbled Horace head-first into the box. 'Canny,' he shouted. 'Listen!' And he tapped again, first on one part that sounded definitely solid, and then in the other corner. 'Hear at?'

'Just like e owld bugger til play tricks on us,' complained Elsie.

'If it's hollow, there must be a way o openan it,' said Wildy Ham. 'It maun be a secret compartment.'

*　　*　　*

Sinclair Cattach was not very happy about having to rise at six o'clock in the morning just to please Bowser Clett. But Bowser had insisted on the hour – in fact he had said three o'clock, but Cattach had beaten him down to six – so that the two of them could remove their invention from the shed and carry it down to the harbour without anyone seeing them, especially without Wildy

Ham seeing them. Bowser had a mortal fear of becoming a laughing stock through Cattach's wild idea to try ranching crabs.

'Put at torch oot!'

'Heaven's sake, Bowser, there's no a war on.'

'I'm a respected member o iss community,' objected Bowser. 'Every chiel kens you're daft, but I'm no in e same category yet. Have ye been drinkan?'

'I had a rum for thermal reasons,' admitted Cattach.

They manhandled the cage through the shed door as easily as they could in the orange glow from the street lamps and laid it flat on the ground. 'It's heavier than I thocht it would be.'

'Once we start movan, it'll seem lichter,' said Cattach.

One at each end of the metal cage, they made their way towards the harbour through the deserted street. Soon they had passed beyond the houses and were making good progress down the slope to the sea.

'We seem til be goan faster,' said Bowser, at the front.

'Doonhill,' said Cattach. 'Gravity is our friend.'

He dug his heels in and slowed their progress, as they reached the level of the quay. 'Have you the stones aboard?' he asked.

'Aye.'

'I hope iss desire for clandestine work doesna mean we're goan til have til row til the sea.'

'Husht.'

'Ye're hearan things.'

Bowser stopped, forcing Cattach to haul back on the cage to avoid pushing his colleague into the harbour.

'Bliddy richt I'm hearan things,' whispered Bowser.

Cattach strained his lugs but, beyond the soft whisper of the waves, he could distinguish nothing.

'Aye, boys, fine nicht.'

The words cut through the darkness with the surprise of a lightning bolt. Bowser dropped his end and Cattach staggered back as the sudden increase in weight nearly cowped him.

'Wildy? Is at ee, boy?'

'Aye, Bowser, it's me all richt, and a sorry state I've fallen intil. Fit's at ee've got ere?'

'Nothing,' said Bowser hastily.

'Well, it's a funny world,' said Cattach with malice.

Bowser adjusted his bonnet, while he desperately tried to think of a good explanation for his strange behaviour. He failed and ended up saying lamely, 'Ee for oot?'

'No til e sea,' said Wildy quietly. 'But I'm oot all richt.'

Cattach and Bowser sensed that their neighbour was not a happy man.

'I'll tell ee fit it is,' said Wildy. 'But I dinna want it til go no further.'

'No,' replied Bowser quickly. 'Understood,' added Cattach.

'It's Ina and Horace,' went on Wildy. 'They've antled on at me at much about at bliddy box o my grandfaither's, at I lost e rag and came doon here for a bit o peace. And fit happens? Ye two turn up. Is there no a quiet corner left in iss world far a man can think in peace?'

'Fit would ye be thinkan about?' asked Bowser cautiously.

'Ye'll have heard about e box. E whole place kens. Lord kens fit my mither and Jess expected til find in it, but it was empty. And then Horace goes and finds iss secret compartment. There was something in it, richt enough.'

'Is at so?' Cattach was suddenly overcome by curiosity and Bowser had to wallop him to remind him this was a delicate situation.

Wildy sighed.

'Aye?' prompted Bowser softly.

'Well, there was a photo in it, o my grandfaither fan he was young, wi some fine-lookan ain on his airm, and a bit o paper. He had written on e paper 'Seek and ye shall find'.

'Is that all at was in it?' asked Bowser. 'Seek and ye shall find? Fit could he mean by at?'

'Oh, he knew fine at Elsie and Jess were at daggers drawn ower his will,' said Wildy in a miserable tone. 'He did it til spite them, I'm sure o it.'

Cattach sat down on the cage. 'D'ye ken the woman in the photo?'

'No, it was taken a while ago.'

'I think this is a mystery,' intoned Cattach. Bowser rolled his eyes: a mystery to Cattach was like a dripping bone to a hungry dog, and the fisherman sensed they were off on another cantraip. Sure enough, Cattach went on, 'There may be a clue in the photo. Would it be possible til have a look at it?'

'Jess has it,' said Wildy sadly.

The prospect of trying to get anything out of Jess Toft, let alone a picture that might be of great significance in the money line, made all three silent for quite a long time. At length Wildy stood up.

'Weel, I'm gettan cowld sittan here. I'm goan home for my breakfast. I micht have til eat it by mysel til get peace. The wife has been infected by my mither's girnane. Stormy weather, boys. Is at some kind o creel?'

'Creel?' echoed Bowser, who had also by this time sat down on the cage and now tried to pretend he hadn't noticed anything unusual. 'Oh aye, it's a keep creel.'

Wildy peered at the so-called creel but he was preoccupied so much by his domestic predicament that he dismissed any thought about its unusual size, shrugged and went away into the darkness.

'He kens,' whispered Bowser anxiously, once the other was out of earshot.

'Seek and ye shall find,' mused Cattach.

'Never heid at. Maybe Toftie died and left them nothing at all. Wildy saw the cage. It'll be all ower e village afore he's finished his breakfast at we're up til something.'

'It's a mystery,' repeated Cattach.

Bowser looked towards the sea. 'I told ee we should have come doon at three o'clock. It's half past six now, and e wind's gettan up.'

*   *   *

Dougie rose at seven o'clock and, after tea and a piece, fed the cattle. Then he released the two calves from the pen in the byre. They bolted to their mothers and suckled greedily. As he pushed a barrowload of dung out towards the midden, he noticed that the wind was rising and beginning to moan around the steading. 'We're in for a gale,' he announced to the dog. Black clouds piled up in the east and heavy rain had begun to slant down. He went back to the house for a coat and Alison met him at the door.

'I think it's coming,' she gasped.

'Aye, it looks like a gale.'

'Not the weather, you gowk,' cried Alison, 'the bairn', and she gasped again.

'Oh Lord!'

'Don't panic. I've got my case ready. But you'd better take me to the hospital.'

*   *   *

Magnus Stroup was finding life a strain. Since Dougie and Alison had rescued him from the paparazzi, he had been trying to keep a low profile. His own account of the incident, only slightly embellished, had been reported in the papers and so far there had been no strong comeback. A fellow councillor in Inverness had phoned him to ask for the Dutch address and his neighbours had been giving him curious looks – whether in contempt or amusement, it had been hard to tell – but that so far had been all he had had to bear. Peggy was making his life a misery at home but he regarded that as a just penance and, to mollify her, had discovered a keen interest in housekeeping and DIY. He was washing the breakfast dishes when the doorbell rang. Muttering, he answered it.

'Oh,' said Dreep when he saw the councillor. 'Are ee busy?'

Magnus hastily removed the floral apron. 'Washing up,' he growled.

'Sorry but I was winderan when I could have anither driving lesson.'

Magnus apologised and said he had been very busy lately. Dreep's grin and rapid nods of agreement distressed the councillor but he made off to find his diary. They fixed a time for the following week.

'Is there anything else?' asked Magnus testily, when Dreep showed no signs of wanting to leave.

'Eh . . . no,' cried Dreep cheerfully. 'Right, cheerio then.'

*   *   *

By mid-morning, when Dougie arrived home, the wind and rain had developed into a full gale. He had left Alison in the hospital and had promised to return as soon as he had fed the sheep and seen to the necessary work on the croft. Turning his back on the spate, he strode out into the park, where the ground sloped down from the hill. A row of large round bales wrapped in black plastic – the store of hay for winter feed – stood along the edge of the brae. He cut plastic from one of them and began to fork out twists of hay, hurrying to avoid the wild weather and thinking of his wife going into labour. He carried hay out to where the sheep were gathering to eat and, as he piled the fodder into the nets, became suddenly aware of a presence.

To his surprise the bales had started to move, pushed by the wind, and as they moved they picked up speed. Two, each weighing seven or eight hundredweight, were trundling down the brae towards him at an alarming rate. He stood transfixed by this unusual sight and by the time he realised what was happening it was too late to dodge them. He turned and started to run but the hay fork dug into the ground and tripped him. He fell flat on his face just as the charging bales caught up with him.

*   *   *

'Wild gale,' gasped Bowser, as he slammed Cattach's door shut behind him. He detached his bonnet, which he had been wearing back to front, and shook the rain from it. The cat, chomping on fish beside the cooker, hissed and growled as the drops of water struck him. This gave the fisherman a pang of pleasure.

'Jean has lost a slate off the shop roof,' said Cattach. 'Mind you, I always thought she had a loose slate or two. Come ben. It's a day for a malt. Is the cage secure?'

'Aye,' said Bowser. 'I covered it wi a tarpaulin and beeg stones so no chiel can see fit it is.'

'I've been on the web,' announced Cattach, fetching a bottle from the press. 'I did a search on crabs. Didna find much except stuff on pets and recipes. They do crab ranching in America but nothing here.'

Bowser watched Cattach pour out two drams. 'I hevna a clue

fit you're speakan aboot. Fitna web?'

Cattach shook his head and recorked the bottle. 'The worldwide web. I'll show you. But you see what it means. We are pioneers.'

Being a pioneer did not have great appeal for Bowser. 'I dinna think iss spells anything but trouble. Hev ee a drop o watter for iss whisky?'

'Seek and ye shall find. No, I dinna mean water.' Cattach went to the kitchen and called back above the noise of the tap. 'I mean Owld Toftie's message. It's a mystery right enough.'

*   *   *

The mystery of Owld Toftie's last message was also plaguing his grandson, Wildy Ham, at that moment. The old mannie's will had now been revealed to the family but it contained nothing out of the ordinary: £500 to each of his two daughters, and that had been about it, a miserable inheritance considering all the rumours about the fortune that the sailor had amassed, by means dubious or otherwise, during his career. The words 'Seek and ye shall find' and the photograph, all they had found in the locked box under his bed, were either a joke or a clue. Wildy could not decide which and he did not want to discuss the possibilities with his wife, his mother or any of his relatives. They were all too busy quarrelling or not speaking with each other. Maybe Cattach could shed some light on the puzzle but, before that could happen, Wildy had somehow to prise the photograph from his aunt's tight grip. He sat musing on this quandary as the rain battered the window and the wind howled around the lumhead.

*   *   *

'Oh, isn't she bonny?' cried the nurse, when she saw the baby in Alison's arms. 'She looks just like you.'

'I think she looks more like her father,' said Alison. 'And I would like to know where he is. He said he would come back as soon as he had fed the sheep. He'll get a piece of my mind when he shows up.'

At that moment, the midwife stuck her head around the door. 'Everything okay, Mrs Bayne?'

'Aye, fine. I'm just knackered.'

The nurse paused. 'Mrs Bayne,' she repeated. 'Eh, well, is your husband a tall man, dark haired?'

'He's going a bit thin on the top but I suppose you could say dark haired.'

The nurse laughed and then stopped herself. 'It's no really funny.' She rose and went to leave the ward. 'Just wait a minute or two.'

It was a good few minutes before the nurse returned and, when she came, she was pushing a wheelchair in which sat no other than the missing husband, looking a bit shamefaced.

'Where have you been?'

'I can explain,' he murmured. 'I got run ower by a bale. See.'

He pointed to his left foot, encased in a gleaming ball of plaster.

The nurse was laughing but recovered enough of her breath to say, 'He was admitted in an awful mess. All gutters and sharn. We knew he was a crofter all right. He's fractured his ankle.'

*   *   *

'Far ee off til in iss weather?' Joy Ham's question had fire in it. Wildy buttoned up his jacket and said the wind was dying down.

'It's gettan dark. It'll soon be your tea.'

'Can I come, Dad?' piped up Billy.

'No, I'll no be long,' said Wildy, and he went out quickly before anyone else could put another question.

*   *   *

'I can hardly get ower iss wee craitur being wirs,' murmured Dougie. He and Alison lay side by side on the hospital bed and gazed at their first-born, wrapped in a blanket and sleeping contentedly in her mother's oxter. 'I fancy Emma.'

'That's a nice name,' said Alison lazily. 'Emma Bayne. Why did you think of that?'

'Dinna ken. My mither was Jessie, yours is Gladys – they dinna seem e thing nowadays. What d'ye think?'

'I was going through the agonies of childbirth, wondering where you had got to, whether you'd had an accident . . .'

'I did have an accident.'

'I meant a road accident,' she laughed.

'I dinna think it's funny til be run ower by a bale o hay. And neither will ee fan I'm hobblan on crutches roond e place an ee'll hev til do all e work. An e lambing'll be startan.'

'Oh, fine. You can stay in and change the nappies.'

'Great. Anither addition til e skitteran army. Maybe Murdoch or Short Bob would lend a hand. We've been feedan four o Bob's sheep all winter. He can pay off his debt. He canna shift them just now anyway, until iss bliddy foot-and-mouth is past.'

A knock sounded on the door of the ward, and it opened to reveal a nurse. 'You're both famous,' she said. 'Here's the press.'

Alecker Munro appeared, managing to look eager and sheepish at the same time. 'Hi,' he said. 'Stay like that. It's a great photo.'

*　　*　　*

Wildy Ham walked slowly along the village street in the dusk, his hands deep in his pockets and his mind deep in thought. He paused as he came near to the house where his Auntie Jess lived, as he didn't want her to see him. He knew, of course, that she spent a good deal of her time surveying the street from the window – not much went off her – but, as it was half-dark and she would be making her tea, he felt he just might get away with not being spotted. Inside her house, probably on the mantelpiece, was the photograph left by his grandfather that he wanted to get his hands on. The simple act of going up to the door and asking for it was impossible. Jess and Wildy's mother, Elsie, had lapsed back into the cold war that had prevailed between the sisters for years; there had been a brief, if hostile, thaw in relations immediately after Owld Toftie's death but that had lasted only for about four days – some had thought this a record.

Wildy leaned against the telegraph pole. No, there was

nothing else for it – he would have to resort to underhand means to snaffle that photo and show it to Cattach who, for once, might turn his brain to useful purpose instead of wasting it on daft schemes. Wildy thought back to when he had been surprised by Cattach and Bowser Clett carrying some contraption down to the harbour. That was another mystery – the purpose of the big cage that Bowser had dismissed as a keep creel. It was plainly no such thing. Brimster was full of mysteries. A movement of the curtain in his aunt's front window snapped him out of his cogitation and he hastily turned away before she could see his face.

As he turned, he almost walked slap into a small boy.

'It's yoursel, Gavin,' he muttered.

'Hi,' said Gavin Leavad, the son of his wife's cousin, Nellie, and one of Jess's grandchildren. The Tofts and the Hams between them accounted for a sizeable proportion of Brimster's population.

'Oh, Gavin?'

'Aye?'

'Are ee goan til your granny's?'

'Aye.'

'Right. At's fine then. Okay, good nicht.' For a moment, Wildy had entertained the mad notion of entering Jess's lair at Gavin's tail. But that was no use – too dangerous. However, Gavin's appearance had planted the seed of another approach in the fisherman's mind.

April

'Proceed along the road until I give you another direction.' Magnus Stroup had adopted his driving instructor's voice, appropriately enough as he was giving Dreep a driving lesson. Dreep drove slowly through the village. 'You can go a little faster,' said Magnus. What was really on the pupil's mind was how he might find out more from Magnus about the Amsterdam brothel, but it was hardly the sort of thing you could just bring up in a driving lesson.

'Speed limit here,' said Dreep. 'Thirty.'

'Well, you'll have to accelerate to reach it,' said Magnus with what Dreep considered unnecessary sarcasm. 'Watch that pedestrian.'

'It's just at reporter chiel, Alecker Munro,' said Dreep.

'What!' Magnus seemed suddenly to lose the place. 'Turn left. Turn left here. Quick, man! Faster!'

Dreep was later to deny that he panicked and turned left too soon. He was to hint that Magnus had jumped on the accelerator on the dual controls and may even have yanked the steering wheel but, however it happened, at that moment they unexpectedly ran out of tarmac and found the nose of the car dipping in an almost genteel fashion into the ditch that ran past the manse.

'What did you think you were doing?' breathed Magnus fiercely. 'Try reverse. No. Reverse! At's third!'

Dreep felt that it hadn't been his fault but kept this opinion to himself. He found the right gear and, in his haste and inexperience, let out the clutch too fast. The car bucked and stalled. Silence hung like a dark curtain as instructor and pupil gazed through the windscreen, across the sloping bonnet, to the manse dyke. Dreep began to wonder if this unexpected halt to his lesson would bring him a rebate.

'Iss is no use!' Magnus released his door but he couldn't push it open very far against the grass of the verge. 'Can ee get oot?'

'Dinna ken.'

'Well, try!'

Dreep tried, but his door opened to provide a gap of only two inches. 'Hing on,' he cried cheerfully. 'I've an idea.'

The idea was the window. Dreep wound it down as far as it would go, wriggled up and managed to worm his way out to fall on the verge, in the process pushing the sole of his left shoe against Magnus's head. Dreep got up and surveyed the car. 'We're stuck right enough,' he announced. 'Oh here's e minister.'

Mr Milton had seen them from his study window and any diversion from writing another sermon was welcome. He came across his garden and leaned over the dyke. A verse from the Book of Matthew came into his head – 'wide is the gate and broad is the way that leadeth to destruction . . .' – and he smiled. 'Do you need a phone?' he asked.

Then a Good Samaritan drove past, in the form of Short Bob on his Fergie tractor. 'I dinna think ee'll get oot o ere,' observed Bob loudly. 'D'ye want a tow?'

'Of course,' bellowed Magnus from his place of imprisonment.

Bob got down laboriously and slowly unwound a thick rope from among the rubbish behind the driving seat. Watching this, the fuming Magnus noticed a row of small, laughing faces along the top of the wall around the school playground.

'I was just gettan some messages before goan til feed Dougie's animals,' said Bob to Dreep, as they sauntered to tie the rope to the rear of the disabled car.

*   *   *

Dougie was practising walking with a crutch, going back and fore across the kitchen. The cast on his left ankle would be there for six to eight weeks, the doctor had said, and he would have plenty of time to become accustomed to his Long John Silver act, as Alison had described his awkward movements in a lengthy phone call to her mother, Gladys, who was presumably at this moment packing her bags before rushing to catch a train north to see her first grandchild. The grandchild, Emma, was being fed by her mother at the kitchen table.

'I've an idea,' said Dougie.

'A motorised crutch?'

'No. Mind ee, at's no a bad idea. No, I was thinkan at, now I'm kinda stuck for a whilie, I micht have time til get til grips wi at computer o yours.' He paused as Emma made some slurping sounds. 'She thinks it's a good idea too.'

'So does her mother,' said Alison. 'I've been at you for ages to do it.'

'We could have a website. Sell produce. How aboot www.neeps.com? We could combine selling – a free handmade pot wi every bag o tatties.'

'Don't remind me. I haven't thrown any pots for weeks.'

Dougie had reached the window. 'Here's Short Bob on his tractor. I wonder fit kept him?'

*   *   *

'Are ee goan oot wi Gavin e day?' Wildy Ham tried to make the question to his son sound casual. The eleven-year-old shrugged: 'Mebbe.'

'D'ye ever go intil his granny's hoose?'

Billy Ham frowned. His granny and Gavin's granny were sisters but he had been forbidden, an injunction frequently repeated by his mother, ever to darken Jess Toft's door. 'No,' he said.

Wildy grunted, thinking. 'Aye, I ken,' he said quietly. 'Weemen are a funny crowd, boy. They take intil their heids no til speak til one anither, sometimes for no reason at all.'

'Mam says Jess wants all e money at great-grandad left.'

'He didna leave very much,' said Wildy hastily. 'They're fechtan aboot nothing. I dinna think we should be bothered wi at.'

Billy waited. His father was up to something.

'There is something he did leave at I would lek til see,' went on Wildy. 'It's just a photo. O your great-grandad when he was a young man. I think it's on Jess's mantelpiece. I mean, it's no worth anything, but there would be no hairm in gettan a lend o it. We can make a copy o it for wirsels.'

'What d'ye want me til do?'

*   *   *

As Dougie emerged from the house, Short Bob laboriously climbed down from the seat of the Fergie. When his feet touched the ground, he paused facing the wheel before straightening and turning. Dougie thought he could have got on the tractor and off again faster, even with a crutch.

'Aye,' said Bob, eyeing the younger man's foot encased in plaster and covered with an old sock, as Dougie's dog, Bess, sniffed around his dungarees. 'At's ee grounded for a while. I'll feed e animals. No bother.'

'D'ye want a cup o coffee before ee start?'

'Weel, I widna say no.'

'Come on in. I'm gettan quicker at movan wi iss prop. Oh, step in at basin, will ee?'

Short Bob stared at the pink liquid in the basin by the door.

'It's disinfectant.'

'Ee'll no catch anything off o me,' protested Bob, but he did as he was told.

'Just a precaution,' said Dougie, 'as long as iss feet-and-mooth is on e go.'

Bob peched as he maintained his balance lifting his heavy boots in and out of the basin. 'Fit's in front o us'll no go by us,' he argued.

'And God helps them at helps themsels,' countered Dougie.

*   *   *

Jess Toft heard the crash when she was dusting in the lobby. She was lifting each ornament and swiping it with the duster, all the time thinking of her late father and the miserable £500 he had left her, and him supposed to have been the owner of a fortune in money, gold and jewels from his days sailing and adventuring around the world. It was all rubbish, she was thinking sourly, all a make-up, but that's what men were like, only good for the one thing, useless fleeps that they were. With her strong left arm she had hefted a brass figure, had scoured its shiny surface and was putting it back when the screech of brakes cut through her girning. Instinctively she shot to the window and peered out through the lace curtain.

On the pavement two bikes had collided. She could see a set of handlebars sticking up in the air and close by it but at such an angle that it had to belong to another bike an arc of wheel, still spinning. As she watched, a boy's head rose into view. 'Gavin,' she breathed, recognising her grandson, 'Fit's at young devil done now?' And she opened the door and hurried down the path, the duster still in her hand.

'Oh Granny,' cried Gavin. 'Billy's hurt himsel.'

'Can ye no watch fit ye're doan, e both o ee?' she flyted. 'Ee go flyan aroond on at bikes wi no thocht. Fit's wrong wi ee?'

Billy Ham sat on the pavement, clutching his shin. Jess saw that the fabric of his jeans was torn and, aye, there was something red and sticky oozing between the boy's fingers. Billy groaned and closed his eyes.

'It's just a scratch,' growled Jess but without conviction. She found herself torn between a natural sympathy for the boy – she was not entirely without sympathy for her fellow creatures, despite rumours to the contrary – and the fact that Billy was the son of her niece and, therefore, a member of the wrong branch of the family.

'It's bleedan,' cried Billy, and he screwed up his face as if he were straining to quench tears.

'He micht bleed til death,' said Gavin with delicious pleasure.

'Haud your tongue,' said Jess. 'At's far fae his hert. He's just skinned his knee.'

Gavin was not to be put off. 'E wound is fill o germs. We should wash it and bandage it at once.'

Jess looked across the street and noted the movement in the curtains on Miss Sarah Job's living-room window. Her instinct was to send Billy Ham away, tell him to go home to bleed on his own kitchen floor, but she thought that she should not appear callous. 'All richt, come in, and we'll see,' she said.

Gavin helped his pal to his feet and supported him as they followed Jess up the path. This was done with a great amount of groaning, moaning and slow limping, and Jess almost lost patience with them, but at last the two boys were in the lobby, hanging on to each other.

'Dinna touch anything,' warned Jess. 'I'll get a cloot.'

When she disappeared into the kitchen, Billy whispered to Gavin: 'I'll get e photo. Keep watch.'

'Hurry up.'

Billy darted into the living room. Gavin waited in terror. Then Billy was back and only remembered to clutch his shin again and sink to the ground when he heard Jess turn off the kitchen tap and return to the lobby.

'I'll do it,' Gavin cried, grabbing the cloth from her hand. 'We had first aid at e school. Hev ee a bandage?'

'A bandage,' repeated Jess in exasperation. 'Ee can make do wi Elastoplast.' Muttering she disappeared towards the kitchen again.

'Get it?' hissed Gavin.

'Aye.'

'I want a share o e treasure.'

*　　*　　*

Magnus Stroup was thinking that life had been hard on him recently. First, the photo in the brothel, second, the foot-and-mouth epidemic had turned all the farmers and crofters who normally bought goods from him into very thrawn customers, and now the shame of being towed from the ditch by Short Bob's tractor while the minister looked on. There was no doubt that being in the public eye had its drawbacks and he felt an instinctive sympathy with the Prime Minister and Madonna.

He stirred his coffee and gazed through the window at the back green. What he needed was some means by which he could restore his public reputation, a bit of positive public relations for once. The opportunities for this in Brimster were limited, he told himself and, lifting a chocolate digestive from the table, he took it and his coffee through to the lounge. Under the weight of his cares, he picked up the remote control and idly flicked on the television. On the News there was another report about the poor prospects for the tourist industry.

'That's it!' he cried, slopping his coffee. 'Tourism. At's what I can do. What can I call it? The Magnus Stroup Heritage Society. No, at's no good – they'll make fun o at. Never heed e name for now. We'll start wi a meeting.'

*   *   *

When the boys had gone, Jess took the Elastoplast tin back to the kitchen and, as she placed it on the shelf, realised that the two youngsters had gone off with the cloth she had given them to wipe the blood from Billy's shin. That's odd, she thought, still it's only an owld cloot. If she could have seen the boys, by this time at the other end of the village, pedalling as if angels flew with them, she might have been very suspicious. Billy and Gavin pedalled all the way home and burst, gasping, into the kitchen of Billy's house.

'What's at on your leg?' Billy's mother, Joy, demanded to know.

'Nothing,' cried her son, and he and Gavin burst into skirls of laughing.

'And I told you before no til keep wearing at pair o torn jeans,' went on Joy Ham. 'Goan oot like a tramp.'

'Far's Dad?' cried Billy.

'At e harbour, I expect.'

The boys cycled down to the sea without any further explanation. They found Wildy Ham working with some creels on the quay. 'Well?' he demanded.

'Here it is,' whispered Billy in a conspiratorial but triumphant tone. He took the photograph from under his jersey and offered it to his father.

'How did ye manage it?'

'No problem. We pretended we were hurt and she took us in. See.' Billy showed the large piece of Elastoplast on his shin, while Gavin pulled the cloth, smeared with tomato ketchup, from his pocket and held it up as further evidence of their ingenuity.

'She didna suspect anything?' asked Wildy cautiously. 'Mind, ee'll be for it if she ever finds oot ee tricked her.'

The boys dismissed the doom-laden prospect. 'Fit aboot e photo?'

'Ye both did well,' said Wildy. 'Come wi me, we'll show iss til a very clever man.'

'Fa?'

'Just stick wi me.' Wildy laid aside the creels and set off back up towards the village.

Sinclair Cattach had not been expecting them so soon. Wildy and the boys filed into the old man's living room. A cat stared and growled. Not finding any seat free from papers the visitors remained on their feet, the boys gazing open-mouthed at the musty paintings and the laden shelves.

'So this is the famous picture,' said Cattach, peering at it. 'Toftie left this and the cryptic message 'Seek and ye shall find'. What does it all mean? Yes indeed, what does it all mean? Well I can tell you something about this picture.'

'Ye ken fa it is?'

'No, the young lady is unbeknownst til me,' admitted Cattach, 'but I ken where it was taken. See that. Don Studios. He was a Brimster man who had a photographic business here between the wars.'

'Ye mean at photo was taken in Brimster?'

'He had a studio in Wick as weel,' explained Cattach. 'Didna do too weel in either place.'

There was a knock at the door. Wildy started. 'If at's Bowser, I'm no here,' he said urgently. 'I dinna want him til ken aboot iss. And if it's Jess, I'm no here either.'

Cattach raised a cautioning hand. 'Let's see,' he advised, and went to the door. While the others waited – Gavin and Billy expectantly, Wildy fearfully, Cattach opened the door by a couple of inches and peered out. His eyes widened when he saw hovering above the step a head with blue hair.

'Mark, it's yourself,' cried Cattach loudly, hoping that his voice would carry from the door to the living room where Wildy and the boys would be listening like hawks and would need reassurance. 'Come away in, another set of brains is just what we're needan.'

As Cattach led the young man ben, Billy and Gavin went into spasms trying to suppress giggling. Wildy merely stared. None of them had seen anyone with blue hair before, certainly not the bright, Saltire-blue that now adorned the head of the minister's son.

'I'm home for a week, so I thought I would gie you a shout,' said Mark Milton cheerfully. 'What's doing?'

'Ah-ha,' said Cattach. 'There you have hit the nail on the heid. Your arrival is indeed timeous. See this photo here.'

Mark studied the somewhat battered photograph while Wildy, collecting his wits, explained it showed his grandfather as a young man with an unidentified, attractive woman on his arm. Cattach added that it had been taken in the long-gone Don Studio in Wick. Mark thought it was interesting but said he didn't know who the people were.

'Oh no, ye wouldna ken them,' agreed Cattach. 'Long before your time. But we think this may be a clue to Owld Toftie's hidden fortune. Now, haud on a minute.'

He went to a bookcase and began to rummage in its contents. Wildy shot an angry glare at his son who, give him his due, was still trying not to see anything amiss in blue hair. Gavin, however, was less polite. 'What's your heid blue for?' he piped up. Wildy was mortified but Mark wasn't the least put out: 'Och I just thought I would try this colour for a change,' he said. Wildy was thrown off balance again when Cattach's old tomcat, a notoriously bad-tempered animal, jumped on to the table and, purring, began to rub contentedly against Mark's hand.

'Here we are!' cried Cattach. 'A map o Wick in the 1930s.'

'Is there nothing ee hevna got in at press?' said Wildy.

Cattach ignored the question and unfolded the map. Then he paused with a look of disappointment on his face – 'There's a hole far e Don Studio was,' he said, and poked his finger through the gap to demonstrate the truth of his finding. 'It's no there now anyway,' added Mark, looking over his shoulder. 'That's where the public toilet is.'

*   *   *

Magnus Stroup almost felt like rubbing his hands with glee as he stepped briskly along the street towards the shop. The ding of the bell above the shop door seemed to him like a peal in salute to his genius, and he presented himself boldly before Jean who, as usual, was lurking behind the till.

'Here's a poster for ye,' cried Magnus.

'Oh aye?' muttered Jean. She unrolled the sheet of paper and read it aloud. 'Public meeting. Brimster Arms. A heritage society for the village. Keynote address Magnus Stroup, Councillor. Discussion to follow.' Jean looked up. 'Is iss yours?'

'Yes.'

'I'll see if I've room for it.'

'Of course ee've got room for it,' spluttered Magnus. 'It's important for wir future, til boost e economy and e tourist trade.'

'Fitna heritage hev we got?'

Magnus hesitated. 'It'll be good for your trade,' he whispered, after a moment's thought.

Jean frowned. 'All richt, then, I'll pit it up.'

*   *   *

'I'm no goan lookan for anything aboot han wi a public lavatory,' said Wildy Ham. 'Besides, how e devil could e owld chiel have buried anything under tarmac, concrete and sewage pipes withoot being catched?'

'Maybe he hid it in e cistern, lek e gun in e Godfather,' suggested Billy, but no one listened to him.

Cattach scratched his head. 'It's a mystery right enough. There's one other thing we could try but I can't guarantee success.' He looked at the others and took their blank stares as assent. 'Right.'

Finding another map, of Caithness this time, he spread it out flat on the table, wiping a dehydrated, compressed slater from the fold as he did so. Then he pulled open a drawer and took out a thin loop of chain with a white object hanging from it.

'This is a shark's teeth,' he announced. 'A very clever man

gave it til me years ago.'

Without further explanation, Cattach leaned over the map and allowed the chain and the dangling tooth to swing gently back and fore over the paper. Wildy's eyebrows dropped in suspicion and he was forced to whisper to Mark: 'Fit e devil is he doan now?'

'I think he's divining,' whispered Mark. 'I've heard o iss but never seen it done.'

The shark's tooth, followed by every pair of eyes in the room, traced out arcs in a slow, graceful way. For ages, it seemed the only sound was the tick of the clock until Cattach cried in triumph and made the others all jump. 'Got it. Stroma, by God!'

'Stroma?' echoed Wildy Ham in disbelief. 'How d'ye ken it's Stroma?'

'That's what the shark's teeth says,' declared Cattach seriously. 'I picked up a definite response when I passed it ower Stroma.'

'It's only a map of Stroma,' pointed out Mark Milton quietly.

'It's supposed til work on a map, I believe,' said Cattach.

'We can go in the boat,' cried Billy.

'Just ye pipe doon,' growled his father. 'And ye'd better get at photo back til your granny before she misses it.'

Billy and his cousin, Gavin, groaned in unison. They felt there was too much happening in Cattach's living room for them to miss. 'Go on,' said Wildy. 'Can we come richt back?' 'All richt then, but hurry up.' 'Dinna do anything withoot us.' With that the boys scuttled out, slamming the door behind them. Wildy sat down and blew a sigh of exasperation through his lips.

'Stroma,' he muttered to the ceiling. 'Are ye tellan me at Toftie hid something on Stroma? He was never far fae e hoose for years afore he died and I never mind him goan ere. If ee was livan a hunder year ago ee'd be a witch. I think we should call iss whole business off.'

Cattach unbent from the map and slowly stood up, the silver chain with the pendant shark's tooth swinging in his hand. 'The man that gave me this swore it worked,' he said. 'I paid a week's supply o Bogey Roll for it. He said he used it to find things that were lost.'

'Divining can produce amazing results,' said Mark in a

consoling tone. 'Try it again. Maybe there was interference.'

Wildy groaned. 'I dinna believe iss. Two grown men, one wi a bus pass and one wi blue hair, and all iss mumbo-jumbo. What am I doan here?'

*　　*　　*

Dougie had got the hang of changing nappies and he chattered away to Emma as he stood above her, expertly wielding talcum powder and tissues. From where he sat at the other end of the table, Magnus Stroup watched with a benign expression.

'Fatherhood suits ee, Dougie,' he said. 'She's a fine wee bairn.'

'I'm telt she looks like me,' grinned the crofter. 'Yes, ye do . . . goo-goo-goo . . . yes, ye do, ye mayna like at but ye do. Say dad.'

'She'll say it soon enough, boy,' grunted Magnus. 'I've two dochters o my own.'

Alison came in, carrying a box. 'Oh hello, Magnus. I thought it was your car. Want a coffee? I'm dying for some caffeine.'

Magnus said that he wouldn't say no. Dougie did up the bairn's clothes and sat down with her on his lap. Alison put cups on the table and, as she prepared the coffee, Magnus explained the reason for his visit.

'So, ye see,' he concluded. 'I think this meeting should throw up a few ideas on how we can use wir heritage til enhance tourism but I think we should start richt away wi ideas before e meeting. What d'ye think?'

Alison suggested something about the body found in the bog last year, and then they thought of old photos. Perhaps they could get enough together to make an exhibition to attract visitors. 'Brimster – land of the bog people – past and present,' intoned Dougie. 'We'll have til do some research. I've got some owld books ben. Read them years ago but I've no looked at them lately.'

'At's e very thing, boy,' said Magnus. 'And Alison, ye can have some o your pots on display. And I thocht maybe we could have a website too.'

'Funny ye should say at,' said Dougie.

*   *   *

'I think that mannie diddled me.'

Cattach's tone sounded so hurt that Mark felt moved to reassure him. 'Maybe it takes practice,' said the minister's son. 'Maybe it's the map. I don't think you should give up just yet. Divining works. There's plenty of evidence for it.' He sat down in the chair recently vacated by Wildy Ham and stroked the cat that had jumped at once into his lap.

'It's a mystery,' murmured Cattach. He held up the silver chain and stared at it as if it had betrayed him. 'Well, we'll see. Anyway, Wildy's given up.' Then he brightened. 'But there is something else.'

'What?'

'Atlantis,' cried Cattach. 'Maybe at's what the teeth was tellan me. D'ye mind me speakan about it at the New Year? I wrote til the *Groat* but it was never printed. You see, I've always had this thocht that Atlantis was near here. Now . . .' and his brow furrowed and he grew increasingly focused as he spoke '. . . now, here's a chance til kill three birds wi one stone. Atlantis, crabs and treasure. Is at no something? Come on, come wi me.'

*   *   *

Bowser Clett stood in the hold of the *Polaris* and listened to Cattach talking at him from the quay. The fisherman was finding it hard not to be distracted by Mark Milton's bright blue hair. From Bowser's viewpoint it looked as if the young man's head was cut off at the eyebrows.

'So, at's it,' Cattach was saying. 'Mark was wondering if you might be making a trippie in the direction of Stroma.'

'Fit d'ye want til go til Stroma for evenow?' growled Bowser. 'Iss is some new theory o yours? May I remind ee at we've got crabs til feed? Oh, does he ken?' The crab-ranching was supposed to be a secret experiment.

'Aye I told him,' said Cattach. 'It's an owld theory o mine, by the way. The one aboot Atlantis.'

'I hevna got time for trippies at iss time o year. In e summer maybe, fan e days are longest.'

Mark broke in: 'Summer would be fine by me. I'll be home again at the end of June.' As he and Cattach ambled back along the quay, he said in a low voice, 'Maybe we should tell him about the shark's tooth and Owld Toftie.'

'No, no,' whispered Cattach. 'At would only worry him unduly. Bowser's a bit highly strung. Atlantis is enough til be going on wi.'

*   *   *

'I'll be glad when I get iss thing off.' Dougie was sliding a wooden ruler up and down inside the plaster cast on his ankle. It was the only way to find relief from the itching of his covered skin. 'My leig's withered aweiy til a stick.'

At the other end of the table, Alison was feeding Emma. The baby emitted a kind of gurgling hiccup. 'She agrees wi me,' said Dougie.

'She thinks it was very stupid of her dad to get run over by a bale of hay in the first place. Now, are you sure you want to call this website neeps.com? Will everybody understand it?'

'Neeps is a perfectly respectable word. It's time it was used more. Besides a bit o humour'll go doon weel wi e public. We can advertise e vegetables on it, and your pots and everything.'

'We have to grow the vegetables first.'

'I'll be on e tractor as soon as I get iss clay pipe off my leig.'

*   *   *

Susan Ham and Karen Toft sat on a dyke in the village. Gavin Leavad stood by them, admiring the tricks that Billy, Susan's younger brother, was attempting on his bike. He was trying to bounce it on and off the kerb, while still remaining upright. After another unsuccessful go, Gavin cried to him to give up.

'I think it's disgusting,' declared Susan.

'Extremely uncool,' agreed Karen. 'Ee'd think grown-ups would have more sense. They're always criticising us.'

'All at fighting ower money.'

The girls were directing their ire at their parents and more especially at their respective grandmothers, who just recently had failed to avoid an encounter in the shop. Their close proximity, squeezed between the refrigerated display cabinet and the rack of postcards, had been too much for both of them, and their self-control had broken down completely. Jess Toft had called her sister a grasping owld B, and Elsie Ham had responded with some comment about Jess's mouth resembling a torn slipper. Naturally their descendants had been black-affronted.

'I want til be rich,' shouted Billy, 'and drive a Mercedes.'

'I'll have an Alfa Romeo,' said Gavin.

'Cars are rubbish,' declared Billy, preparing for another bounce.

'Shut up, ye two,' said Karen. 'Ye're as bad as wir grannies.'

Gavin grinned at her. 'Karen loves Mark,' he sang. 'Karen loves blue hair.'

'I'm bored,' said Susan. 'I want til do something.' She girned for a moment and then jumped to her feet. 'I know. Let's go and get Amethyst Dean's autograph.'

'She's rubbish,' cried Billy. He was ignored.

'Is she home?' asked Karen.

'Aye. Did ye no see e helicopter? She's at Brimster Hoose again. Let's go and visit her.'

The popstar used Brimster as a retreat and no one had ever seen her in the village. It was well known that she had a mad minder who had stopped Pogo and Dreep from snaring rabbits near Brimster House.

'She'll no let us in,' said Gavin.

'We're fans,' argued Susan. 'We can go straight up til e front door and ask for her autograph. All she can do is say no.'

'Or she micht say yes.' The prospect of success seized Karen and suddenly she was all for going. 'I'll get my mam's CD for her til sign. And a poster.'

'We'll come too.'

'Oh no ye won't, Billy Ham!'

'We'll all go,' said Susan. 'Come on. It's no far. Billy, ye and Gavin, can give us a lift on your bikes.'

Billy and Gavin paused to consider the implications of this idea. But older sisters and cousins have a habit of getting their way and,

with the girls balanced precariously on the seats of the bikes, the boys pedalled off down the road. They wobbled past the hotel but by the time they reached the village hall, where Shirley the hall-keeper was pinning up a notice about the forthcoming meeting on heritage, their balance had improved. Laughing and shouting to each other, they went quickly along the main road.

Pedalling more slowly after covering two miles, Billy and Gavin steered through the pillared gateway to Brimster House. They passed the sign that said 'Private – No Admittance' and tackled the potholed drive. Susan, perched behind her brother, was nearly jolted off when the bike went over a rough piece and cried out to be canny.

'Maybe this is no such a good idea,' peched Gavin.

'Cowardie,' cried Karen.

'I'm knackered wi ee as a passenger. It's time ee lost weight.'

Karen took her hand from her cousin's waist long enough to hit him a wallop on the back of the head. Gavin yelled and lost control. The bike skittered sideways and came to rest against a clump of whins. Karen of course fell off and set up a wailing. 'I'm all purred,' she screamed, 'I'll give you a hammering, Gavin Leavad.' She grabbed a handful of shingle and threw it at him, and it darted off the bike with pinging noises. Then she struggled to her feet and muttered that she would walk the rest of the way.

'Suits me,' shouted Gavin and he pedalled off, with Billy and Susan in close pursuit. Karen ran after them shouting to them to wait but, before she caught up, they had reached the garden of the House.

The gleaming metal gate was shut. There was another sign on it – this time it read 'Strictly Private'. The youngsters hesitated and tried to see over the bedraggled hedge. Susan announced that they should go in and she pushed open the gate. Leaving the bikes against the dyke, the others scuttled after her. On the door hung a huge knocker in the shape of an eagle's beak. They scrutinised this intimidating object.

The door opened and they all stepped back hurriedly when a large man in a shirt and tie appeared suddenly before them. He was not smiling. 'What do you lot want?' he asked sternly. 'This is a private house.'

'Aye, we ken . . . I mean, we know,' said Susan bravely. 'We thought that we would welcome Amethyst Dean til Brimster and . . .'

'We think she's great,' interrupted Karen.

'Aye, we do,' gushed Gavin. 'Eh, are ye Trevor?'

Trevor, if that was his name, was not persuaded to be kind. 'This is a private house. You're all trespassing. Now, be smart kids and . . .'

'Oh, they must be some of Amy's fans.' This was said by a willowy, dark-haired young woman who had materialised at Trevor's elbow.

'Oh yes, miss, we are,' cried Susan. 'We was just wantan her autograph. We think she's fab.' And she produced a CD from inside her anorak.

The willowy woman eased Trevor to one side. 'Oh isn't that sweet. You've all come all this way, and you look as if you had an accident . . .' Karen blushed and started to pick pieces of whin from her jeans. '. . . Well, you'd better come in and we'll see what we can do for you. It's all right, Trevor, there's only four of them.'

Trevor pulled a sour face and shrugged. The four on the pavement gaped.

'Well, come on, then, before I change my mind.'

May

Magnus was feeling chuffed with himself, as he stood in the lounge bar of the Brimster Arms and watched the villagers assemble for the meeting. It was a fairly good turn-out and, judging by the crack at the bar, they all seemed in a benign mood. Magnus glanced at his watch. Give it another five minutes, he decided, and I can call them to order.

Sinclair Cattach was there of course; he would never miss an event like this. The minister had put in an appearance and stood with an orange juice beside the fireplace. Magnus thought that the minister's son, Mark, might have done better than dye his hair blue but, as a councillor, he acknowledged the young man's democratic choice. And there was Dougie, walking on a stick, nursing his healing ankle; and Dreep; and Jean from the shop, with a glass of sweet stout, and Miss Sarah Job. Oh aye, it was a good turn out, right enough. This could be an historic moment, the founding of the Brimster Heritage Society. Magnus smiled as he thought it might prove just historic enough to attract an OBE but then decided he should expect nothing like that, he was only doing his duty by the place, and, forbye, it would help people to forget about the recent unfortunate episodes in his life.

'Aye, Magnus,' he heard someone call, 'I'm lookan forward til your holiday snaps.'

Well, perhaps Amsterdam might take a bit more work, Magnus thought to himself sadly. Still, onward and upward. He glanced at his watch again. There might just be time to get in another dram before the meeting.

'Mr Stroup, Mr Stroup!'

Bearing towards him, gasping a little, came an elderly woman on a Zimmer. She had glasses with thick lenses, and hanging from the Zimmer frame was a crocheted cloth bag.

'Lady Roster,' said Magnus, mustering as much good humour as he could.

'Gillian. Cut out that Lady Roster nonsense. I'm glad I caught you before the meeting. Do you have a moment? I saw your notice and I think this is an excellent initiative of yours.'

She bent and began to rummage in the cloth bag. 'I've got some ideas for you that I think you'll like. All kinds of stuff on the history of Brimster. I've drafted a brochure. Now, where did I put it?'

Magnus suddenly felt an urgent need to start the meeting. 'Eh, aye, fine, Gillian. I'll see it later. We're just kicking off.' Frantically he began to tap the side of a glass with his pen.

'I haven't seen Lady Roster for many a long day,' whispered Miss Sarah Job to Jean, as they sat in the back row at the meeting. 'I thought she was dead.'

'Not her,' said Jean. 'Look at her on at Zimmer. She's still livan in yon big, draughty hoose.'

The object of their interest had fortunately taken a seat in the front row, right under Magnus's nose, so they could watch her and still appear to be listening to the proceedings.

'She's hardy,' muttered Sarah. 'Somebody must have given her a lift. Her man's no wi her.'

'Is he keepan weel?'

'Well, I noor heard if he wis deid yet. He keeps bees.'

Magnus had called for questions or comments from the floor, and people were putting forward some ideas on things the village could do to attract more tourists. Considerable support was voiced for a tea-room and a public convenience. 'There must be something for fowk til look at if id's rainan,' said someone, and the idea of having an exhibition of photos of the body found in the bog went over well. Cattach mentioned sea-angling and historical excursions.

'Well, there's plenty til be thinkan aboot here,' concluded Magnus, beaming. 'The next thing is at we should set up an amenities committee til progress what we've discussed, and go for grants and so on. No a big committee,' he went on hastily, after a glimpse of Lady Roster's smiling countenance, 'just maybe four or five til get things movan.' Mr Milton, the minister, and Donnie

Gill, the headteacher, were called on to be tellers.

Magnus called for nominations and was pleased when Tom Manson suggested that Magnus himself should be chairman. A few other names were eventually secured. Gillian, Lady Roster, began to show signs of agitation in the front row, looking around at the others, struggling with a great rustling of the plastic mac she wore to attract the chairman's eye. If a Zimmer could ever have been stamped, it looked as if it would have been then, but Magnus quickly closed the nominations, and the Heritage Amenities Committee was formally born.

'Mr Stroup,' Lady Roster found her voice. 'I want to show you this.' She rummaged in her bulging cloth bag but seemed to have difficulty in finding what she was looking for. 'Hold on a minute. I must clear out this rubbish some day. Hold that, will you?'

Magnus found himself standing with a half-eaten apple, a piece of bicycle chain, what looked like a manila envelope from the Inland Revenue, assorted door keys and a cairngorm brooch in his hands, and wondered how this had happened. Lady Roster brightened and raised her head from the maw of the bag. She thrust at the councillor a large creased envelope.

'This is a brochure I've written about the history of Brimster,' she declared. 'See what you think. It needs photographs.'

Magnus handed Lady Roster's other possessions back to her and she dropped them all into the bag without a glance. Opening the envelope, Magnus drew out several sheets of paper covered in handwriting. 'That's very good,' he commented. 'Most interestan. E committee'll look at iss. Eh, Dougie!'

Dougie turned on hearing his name. Lady Roster looked at him: 'Me on a Zimmer and you on a stick. We're a couple of old crocks. You're a Bayne.'

Dougie admitted that he was, and Lady Roster grunted in a satisfied way. Magnus said this was Lady Roster, to which she spluttered that her name was Gillian. Edging away from the Zimmer and praying that the old biddy would get it into her head that it was long past her bedtime, Magnus began to explain in a loud and slow voice to Dougie about the interesting brochure.

Alison switched on the electric wheel and watched it for a moment as it spun and hummed. It seemed like ages since she had made a pot and she was looking forward to practising her craft again. Emma was asleep in the cot by the window. Alison poured some water onto the wheel, took up a lump of fine clay, slapped it down hard on the spinning plate and began to fashion it into a shape, enjoying the touch of the material on her hands.

'Hello!'

Alison looked up. Leaning against the jamb of the open door was a slight figure, a woman with short, blonde hair, wearing jeans and a red waterproof.

'Sorry, I didn't hear you,' said Alison. 'Come in. Would you like to look around?'

'I'm disturbing you,' said the newcomer.

'It's just that I was concentrating,' explained Alison.

'I know how it is. Oh, I'm Amethyst, by the way. Your new neighbour, I suppose.' So this was the famous pop singer, Amethyst Dean, thought Alison, of course she should have known that elf-like face at once but, somehow, in real life it looked smaller, more ordinary. She was holding out her hand. Alison showed her palms dripping with brown clay.

'This all your work?' asked Amethyst, moving along the display shelf where Alison's pottery was laid out for inspection and sale. 'Oh I like that one. Can I buy one?'

'Well, yes, sure.' The potter was annoyed at herself for being suddenly flustered and began to wipe her hands on a towel. Emma chose that moment to wake and announced this fact to the world with a protesting cry.

*   *   *

'So, she bought three pots,' explained Alison. 'I've not sold so many at one go this year yet. She's quite nice, you know, not at all stuck-up or contemptuous of us lesser mortals. She loved Emma, watched me change her nappy.'

'Well, I hope she comes back,' said Dougie. 'Goodness alone kens when we're goan til see anither customer. Ye'd think at wi e feet-and-mooth passan folk would start appearan again.'

'And what's more. She's invited us up to Brimster House. Well, not exactly, but she did say drop by any time we are passing.'

'Safe enough. We're never passan up ere. Nobody is ever passan up ere.'

'She told me a bunch of kids from the village came to the door once and asked for her autograph. She thought they were so cute and polite.'

'They must have behaved better than they usually do. I widna ken fit til say til her. I've never listened til her songs and I canna make oot e words anyway. I think ee better go ere yoursel.'

June

Peggy Stroup pricked up her ears. Her husband was on the phone but suddenly there was something curious and false about his voice. She sometimes wondered if her man had started to turn simple and had even thought once or twice that maybe he had always been like that but she hadn't noticed. She rose and went to the door leading through to the small room Magnus used as an office.

'This is Magnus Stroup, councillor. I'm sorry there's no one here at the moment but if you could leave a message I'll get back to you as soon as possible,' her husband was intoning into the mouthpiece.

'What the devil ee up til?' hissed Peggy.

Magnus turned a plea-laden, sorrowful face towards her and held his finger to his lips but kept listening to the phone. A high-pitched squeaking voice penetrated to Peggy's hearing but she couldn't distinguish the words. The voice went on for several minutes, far too long for anyone to expect Peggy to control her impatience and, by the time Magnus put the phone down, she almost spat at him: 'What are ee pretendan til be an answeran machine for?'

'Sorry, darling, it's self-defence,' said Magnus with a contrite expression. 'That was Lady Roster again. That's e fifth time e day at she's phoned me til go on and on aboot at bliddy brochure o hers for e heritage. She's just spent five meenads tellan me how she canna stand answeran machines.'

'Next time let me talk til her.'

'I'm no sure at's a good idea.' The thought of what Peggy could say gave Magnus pause. 'She's just nuts. Just anither o the burdens o office a man in public life has til carry.'

*   *   *

'Dreep, we're a man short. Torquil got lifted by e bobbies on e road home. He was ower e limit. There's a spare kit ere. Get it on, man.' The skipper of the Brimster football team was desperate, or at least desperate enough to ask Dreep to play.

'I'm no sure, I'm no keen,' protested Dreep. 'Besides I've got an injury.'

'No, ee hevna,' cried Pogo. 'No, he hesna, he's just shy. He always underestimates his talent.'

It was a fine evening, and even a few adults had turned out to join the bairns and the dogs to see the locals play a visiting team. Dreep was conscious that everybody seemed to be looking at him but, Pogo was right, he was not keen.

'Fit aboot ee yoursel?' said Dreep to his friend.

'Well, we're no that desperate,' murmured the skipper. 'Hurry up, e ref's aboot til blow for e kick-off.'

'Go on,' urged Pogo. 'This is your big chance. There's nothane til id. All you're doan is makan up e numbers. They're goan til loss anyway. Just run aboot and look as if ee ken fit ye're doan, and try no til do toe-pointers.'

Dreep was finally persuaded. 'All richt then, but I'm no wearan shorts.'

'Longs'll be fine.'

Two minutes later, Dreep emerged from the back seat of the Cortina where he had hastily changed, sporting the team shirt of Brimster Rangers and, to a ragged, maybe sarcastic, cheer from the scattered spectators, hirpled to the sideline and embarked on what Pogo swore would be his ninety minutes of glory.

He didn't do too badly in the beginning, or no worse than his team mates. The visitors scored twice in the first fifteen minutes but then lost puff and the game settled into a kind of aimless loose mêlée in mid-field. Dreep got his second wind and began to feel better. He even kicked the ball three times and once made a pass that raised a cheer. He was beginning to think that maybe he had a gift after all.

When the opposing goalie palmed a wild shot from the Brimster striker around the upright and the ref blew for a corner, the skipper signalled to Dreep to join the forwards in the penalty area. 'Ee sure?' asked Dreep.

'Aye, we've got til go for a goal before half-time. All-out effort.'

There was a lot of jostling and shirt pulling and elbow work in the box, as the players pranced in anticipation of the cross. Dreep felt a hand on his belt. This was too much. 'Keep your hands til yoursel,' he roared, turning to see who was causing the bother. Then he felt a crashing blow on the back of his head and the world went black. When he recovered his senses, he became aware of two things – a forest of legs and boots around him, and a distant wave of noise. Then he realised he was lying face down on bare earth. Shaking himself, he made to get up and suddenly found several pairs of arms helping him to his feet.

'Well done, Dreep. That was fantastic, boy!'

At first he was too confused to ask what he had done that was fantastic, but gradually as he straightened and hands continued to thump him on the back, he understood. He had scored a goal. The other members of the Brimster Rangers were now congratulating him and hustling him away from the goal mouth towards the centre of the field. Cheering rose like a wave from the scattered spectators.

'Brilliant header, Dreep,' shouted the team skipper, clapping his hands. 'Come on, now, boys. We can do it.'

Dreep smiled and accepted all the praise – he was even aware of an incredulous Pogo standing on the touchline – and pieced together what had happened. The ball had struck him on the back of his nut and had glanced into the net. Maybe I am better than I thocht, he thought.

His contribution during the rest of the game was not so spectacular, although he played with the confidence and enthusiasm of the convert. The half-time whistle left the Brimster players feeling jubilant and the visiting team a bit puzzled by the sudden, ominous change in the character of a bunch they had expected to walk over. Dreep sucked on his half-orange as if it were caviar. In the second half Brimster scored again and their goalie even found enough reserves of inspiration to enable him to keep their opponents from putting the ball past him. The final result, a draw at two–two, marked a better performance by Brimster Rangers than anyone watching could remember, and there was even talk of a new dawn.

'Hey, we'll hev til get a pair o shorts if you're goan til be in e team fae now on,' declared Pogo to Dreep in the Brimster Arms afterwards.

'No,' said Dreep slowly. 'I think I did all right but gettan shorts would be goan too far at iss stage. I only got on e team because Torquil was catched and couldna get here in time. Maybe I'll just stay a reserve. Efter all, I think it was more a lucky goal.'

Torquil, the errant midfield player, had already turned up and explained his misfortune to his celebrating team mates. At an office party, he had imbibed too much and had fallen foul of a speed trap on the way home. A court appearance was in prospect, and he was now being congratulated on achieving this rite of passage.

'Well, iss is wir lucky day,' cried Pogo. 'I'm goan til chance a scratch caird.'

*   *   *

Pogo's luck held, which was more than could be said for his ability to contain his liquor. The scratch card had secured him a £10 note and, before they had left the pub, it had been spent. Reeling, he and Dreep took to the street.

'I'm knackered,' muttered Dreep. 'At football takes a lot oot o ee. See ee tomorrow.'

They parted. Pogo made his way alone down the road. It was a fine summer's night. The sky was a soft pale grey and the wind had died away to a soothing breeze. The gentle wash of the surf could be heard from the shore, and it drew Pogo's attention seawards like a siren song. Somehow, though, it was easier to walk downhill and instead of following the road to the harbour Pogo found himself taking the other road that dipped to cross the burn.

'No goan hom yet,' he decided when the upward gradient on the other side of the bridge loomed before him, and he turned onto a footpath that ran beside the burn on its way to the sea. He knew the path well enough and made progress through the

clumps of whins and patches of reeds until he neared the shore.

Here he tripped on something and fell. He lay for a while on his back on the grass. There was still some of the day's heat in it and he felt comfortable at first, but then his head began to ache and a thirst came on him.

'E wellie!' he suddenly said aloud, remembering.

Old wells survived around Brimster as they did throughout the county. Like the others, this one had been neglected for decades but the spring water it tapped still seeped from the ground and flowed to the beach, its progress marked by a bright, lush carpet of wild plants. Pogo went over to the well, knelt above it and peered into the dark, stone cistern at its heart.

'Och it's likely all richt,' he said, and he flattened himself over the rim of the well, and lowered his head until first his nose and then his lips touched the cool water.

*   *   *

'I'm tellan ee, it was miraculous.' Pogo was growing annoyed because Lang Tam and Dreep remained unimpressed by what he was telling them. He repeated the story.

'I was feelan pretty rough and then I took a drink fae e well and, when I wakened up, it was as if I was reborn, I never felt better in my life.'

Lang Tam swung the steering wheel of the scaffie cart to turn the corner onto the main road through Brimster. 'Any drunk chiel feels better efter a sleep,' he growled.

'But I had no hangover,' protested Pogo.

'All at proves is at ee didna have enough before ee fell asleep.'

'Ee dinna believe me but I'm tellan ee, at was no ordinary watter.'

'Fill o dirt, I would think,' said Dreep. 'At owld well's no been used or cleaned for years.'

They got down to manhandle the wheelie bins. After they had wrestled the first two into place at the rear of the vehicle and as they waited for the tipping and emptying, Pogo leered at his mate: 'Besides at's no all.'

'No all what?' said Dreep absently.

'I had a vision.'

'Eh?'

But Pogo didn't answer. He kept a wide, knowing grin on his face until they were both back in the cab. 'Well?' demanded Dreep.

'I'm no tellan ee because ee dinna believe me.'

'Fitna vision? Fit d'ye mean?'

'Television?' asked Lang Tam, but Dreep ignored him.

'I'm no tellan ee,' went on Pogo triumphantly. 'Ee dinna deserve til ken. It's my own personal vision, at's all.'

They drove up the road, stopping at the bins and emptying them, and eventually came to Magnus Stroup's bungalow. Here there was something that took their minds off whatever thoughts were already sifting through their heads. Magnus was at his front door talking to, or rather listening to, a plump old woman on a Zimmer.

'Oh ho,' cried Lang Tam. 'Wir brave councillor is in trouble again. Gillian's up and aboot early e day. I wonder fit she's complainan aboot now.'

Dreep and Pogo got down to do the bins. Dreep pushed one to the back of the cart. 'Come on,' he shouted to Pogo, but Pogo was standing, ignoring his work and obviously lugging in carefully to the doorstep conversation. Gillian, Lady Roster, had a loud, penetrating voice and Pogo's curiosity was easily satisfied.

'Look here, Mr Stroup,' she was saying, 'You're a very difficult man to get hold of. I'm been phoning you constantly and only getting an answering machine. I hate these blasted things. I'm not talking to a device at my age. So, I dug out the old jalopy and decided the only thing to do was to see you. Now, see here . . .' And she dug into the cloth bag hanging from the Zimmer frame. '. . . I've brought you a revised draft of my brochure. This is just the thing for your Heritage Society, something for tourists to pick up. They always want something to pick up . . .'

'Come on,' said Dreep urgently. 'Tam's champan at e bit.'

'Aye, aye,' muttered Pogo. 'Just a meenad.'

Lang Tam stuck his head from the window. This, for him, unusually energetic gesture showed his impatience. 'Are ee goan til stand ere e whole bliddy day?'

They climbed in, paying no attention to Tam's muttering about the inadvisability of lazing on the job outside the councillor's house.

'Well, well,' declared Pogo with a grin. 'Fancy at. Cattach's no e only chiel wi ideas roond here.'

He refused to explain what this might mean and, after a few minutes, Dreep and Tam gave up trying to worm anything like sense out of him.

*   *   *

Alecker Munro parked as near to the open front door of the Lodge as the jungle of bushes would allow and went across the unweeded gravel to push the brass bell button. There was no sound. 'Hello,' he shouted, but his announcement only echoed in the hall he saw through the door. A pair of uncleaned rubber boots leaned against a wooden settle. Leaves had blown in and were scattered across the carpet, and from the look of them some had been there since last autumn.

'She did say three o'clock,' muttered Alecker. He checked his watch and it confirmed he was on time. 'I'll try the garden.'

Lady Roster had phoned and summoned him with the bait of

an interesting story. He didn't think it could be anything much but there was no harm in giving her a half-hour and he had arranged for a friend to phone him at three-thirty to provide an excuse to depart if he needed one.

He went round the corner into the main garden and nearly walked straight into a ladder. A loud buzzing filled the air. Alecker waved a bee away from his face and followed the ladder upwards with his eye to find a tall man perched on the top. The journalist opened his mouth to speak but his jaws froze and no sound came out. The tall man was reaching with his bare arm into an enormous, dark, squirming mass of bees clustered under the rhone.

'Oh Mr Munro,' Lady Roster's voice snapped Alecker's attention back to ground level. 'Come away inside where we can talk. Sherry?'

'But . . .' began Alecker.

'Pay no heed,' said Lady Roster briskly. 'My husband's catching a swarm, that's all, happens all the time in summer.'

Alecker looked up again and saw old Roster's face beaming down at him through a cloud of bees.

'You look as if you've never seen bees before,' said Lady Roster, tapping with her Zimmer. 'Come along, come along. May be you don't need a sherry, but I'm gasping.'

She led the way into the lounge at a snappy pace. 'Find a chair,' she commanded. Alecker looked around at the clutter, the papers, books, bric-a-brac and odd pieces of furniture and finally noticed a battered armchair that seemed free from hazard. As he sat down and as it gave way under him with a creak, he noticed two television sets, one sitting on the other. He was wondering why Lady Roster needed two, when she barked did he want a sherry.

'Well, aye, thanks,' he said, and fumbled in his pocket to find his notebook. 'What was it you wanted til tell me about?'

Lady Roster turned from the drinks cabinet with a glass of sherry and told him to fetch his own, as she needed one hand for the 'blasted apparatus' as she called the Zimmer. It took Alecker a bit of an effort to pull himself up from the chair. 'The springs went west in 1967,' said Lady Roster unhelpfully.

'Now,' she went on, 'what I want to do is light a fire under Magnus Stroup, set off a squib under his backside. He's dragging his feet, you know, over this heritage thing. I don't know why but he's playing hard to get. You know about my brochure?'

Alecker had just tasted his sherry, which he found remarkably mellow, and said nothing.

'Have you heard of the Holy Well of Saint Erik?' asked Lady Roster.

'No, Lady Roster,' he said.

'Gillian, none of this lady nonsense. You haven't? What kind

131

of journalist are you?' She took a swig of sherry. 'No one knows where it is, but the records say there was a well dedicated to the holy geezer in Brimster. It was a place of pilgrimage and healing before the kirk elders had their way. I think I've found it. That's the story.'

At that moment, old man Roster came in, smiled, said nothing and went to help himself to the sherry. He poured one and sat down on a hard chair as Alecker eased himself again into the armchair. Old Roster grinned benignly. Alecker glanced at him and saw a honeybee crawl out from under his shirt collar and fly off towards the open door.

'Eh, yes?' said Alecker.

'I've found it, I'm sure of it,' went on Gillian. 'I'll take you to the place.'

'Who was Saint Erik?' asked Alecker meekly.

'Some Norseman who gave up pillaging and raping and saw the light. He did the usual kind of miracle and became revered in these parts. Never mind him. It's the well. Don't you see what it means? Get the halt and the lame coming here in charabancs, and Brimster's tourist trade will never look back.'

'I understand the plan,' said Alecker, 'but why not put it before the Heritage Committee?'

'Useless lot! Magnus Stroup has no imagination. If you publicise the well, they'll be forced to do something, don't you see?'

'We'll need a photographer. For a picture of the well, with yourself beside it.'

'My phiz in the paper? Well, it's all in the cause. Can you set it up?'

*   *   *

The Heritage Amenities Committee held a meeting that very evening in the lounge bar of the Brimster Arms.

'I'm sorry to report there has been another delay in the plans for the new public toilet facilities,' announced Magnus, the chairman.

'No again,' groaned Jean from the shop. 'How can we get

fowk til come if there's no place for them til go?'

'I ken, I ken,' said Magnus sorrowfully. 'Now, Lady Roster's brochure. Ye've all seen it. Are we goan til get it printed?'

Sinclair Cattach said he had found it a very interesting document but there were one or two errors in it that he would like to check. Magnus said he would in the meantime get some estimates from printers and a decision on the fate of the brochure was deferred to the next meeting.

At the close of the meeting, Cattach spotted Wildy Ham in the public bar and sidled over to him. Wildy eyed the old man suspiciously.

'Fit's new?' asked Cattach.

'Feint a thing,' said Wildy.

'At's e way,' said Cattach, after a brief pause.

They exchanged looks and Cattach gave a wry grin as Wildy drained his nip, slid off the bar stool, said 'We'll be seean ee, boys' and went out. Cattach nodded to himself. So, nothing had changed with regard to solving the mystery of what Toftie might have left to his heirs.

Pogo saw Dougie having a pint and touched him on the elbow. 'Can I hev a word?'

'Surely, fit's doan?' said the crofter.

Pogo's eyes swept left and right before he leaned close to Dougie and whispered, 'It's kinda private lek.'

Dougie's first thought was that Pogo was on to some ploy involving poaching but the scaffieman surprised him by asking in a low voice if Alison was making pots again. Dougie nodded.

Pogo leaned even closer. 'Dinna say anything but could she make peedie pots? So high?' And he held his fingers to indicate something the height of a cup.

'I suppose so,' said Dougie. 'D'ye want a pot lek at?'

'I reckon a hundred would do,' whispered Pogo. 'At first.'

Dougie's expression registered surprise.

'Aye, I ken,' smiled Pogo. 'I'll explain everything later on, but just for now keep it til yoursel. Magic watter.'

*   *   *

'Magic water?' said Alison. 'What on earth does he mean? I know this place is full of crazies, but – tell me this is a joke.'

'I dinna think Pogo was jokan,' said Dougie. 'He seemed pretty excited til me. He wants a hundred pots.'

'I'm not running a factory here,' protested Alison. 'A hundred handmade pots would cost him. Tell him they are two pounds each, and that'll test how serious he is.'

Dougie girned. 'I think we'll just forget it, unless he brings it up again.'

Alison picked up Emma and headed for the door. 'Well, I'm off to visit our resident pop idol. It's a fine day, and Emma and me are going to walk across the hill to see Amethyst Dean in her lair. Can you pick me up later?'

Dougie agreed he could drive round in a few hours' time, and his wife and daughter set off. As she went up the track to the moor, Emma wide-eyed and sun-bonneted in the carrying frame on her back, Alison mused on what Pogo could be up to but reached no conclusion. She went on up to the high ground. Larks were singing and in the gully of the hill road between the clumps of whins, yellow with blossom and loud with bees, the sun was warm.

After a little time, she spotted the roof of Brimster House before her, beyond the crest of the moor, and quickened her pace.

*   *   *

Meanwhile, Magnus Stroup was concluding a driving lesson with Dreep. 'I think you're ready til take your test,' the councillor was saying. 'Your driving's fine, as long as you think what you're doan. It would be better if you could do the three-point turn in less than seven points but at least you didna hit anything or go in e ditch. Now, how's your Highway Code?'

'Oh pretty good,' said Dreep confidently.

Magnus opened his book of road signs and flipped up a picture of a car falling towards wavy lines. 'Fit's at ane?'

'At means ye've just missed e *Ola*,' grinned Dreep.

Magnus groaned. 'Dinna be smart wi e examiner. It's quayside or river bank, and nothing else. Ever!'

'I ken,' said Dreep. He gave the correct responses to the other symbols Magnus flashed before him, and the councillor appeared satisfied.

When Dreep had paid for his lesson and had disappeared down the village street, Magnus moved round the car to reach the driver's side and was about to get in when a loud psst! made him jump. He turned and saw Pogo's head peering from behind a clump of nettles.

'Magnus, hey! Hev ee got a meenad?'

'Fit ee doan ere? Fit is it ee want?'

Pogo emerged from his hiding place and looked about him. Satisfied no one was watching them, he came closer and began to whisper.

'I canna make oot a word ye're sayan. Ee'll hev til speak up,' complained Magnus, irritated.

'Magic water,' repeated Pogo. 'I've got a great idea. Listen, ee ken how every chiel in e toons is keen on trendy stuff til drink. Well, I've found e very thing for them. They'll pay us a fortune for it.'

'I haven't a clue what you're on about.' When Magnus was annoyed he reverted to English. 'Now I'm a busy man.'

'No, haud on.' Pogo gripped the lapel of the councillor's blazer, and Magnus could see what he took to be a mad glint in the other man's eye. 'All richt, it's no magic but it tastes bliddy good and we could market it wi clever slogans and fancy pots. Brimster Spring Water. The Elixir o e North.'

To the dumbstruck councillor, he went on to explain how he had drunk from the old well at the shore and how his hangover had disappeared instantly. Magnus's eyebrows dropped and Pogo could see his listener was now paying some attention.

'Fitna well?'

'E owld well at e shore. I'll show ee. Come on. Ye can taste it for yoursel.'

'I'm busy.'

'Oh? Weel, maybe later on then, but dinna tell any chiel.'

Magnus bent to enter the car but then straightened up. Maybe Pogo wasn't off his perch after all. Spring water and mineral water were big items in trendy bars and restaurants and if the well at the shore did produce the right stuff, and there was no reason why it shouldn't, Brimster could be sitting on a good deal. Magnus had a vision of a bottling plant and a peedie shop, no, a big shop, selling bottles of water to the world. It was his duty as a councillor to develop the resources of the village.

'I can spare ee half an hour, no more,' he said solemnly to Pogo. 'I'll pick ee up at five o'clock and we'll have a look at this well of yours.'

*　　*　　*

Dougie looked wistfully at the large knocker in the shape of an eagle's beak on the front door of Brimster House. It seemed too forbidding a thing to use and he chose to rap with his knuckles. Under the force of his hand, the door swung open a little. 'Hello,' he shouted into the echoing hallway. No response. He took a step inside and called again. A distant voice that he recognised as his wife's came from somewhere: 'We're in here.'

'Far's here?' Finally he found another open door and a bright lobby leading to the kitchen. He had never been inside the rambling, maze-like innards of the House before, and the size of the kitchen brought him up short to stare at the high ceiling, the cupboards, the immense black range and the long table where Alison sat with Amethyst Dean. Emma was asleep in a chair. 'Oh, ye're ere,' he said.

Introductions over, Amethyst offered him a drink. Dougie had never been face to face with a pop star before and he didn't know quite how to react. Will she be offended if I dinna ask for

her autograph? he wondered. He noticed that Alison was holding a mug of something and got out of his predicament by saying 'I'll take e same.'

The same was instant coffee. The pop idol poured it for him and said, 'You're a crofter. That's great.'

Nonplussed, Dougie sipped and smiled. The conversation, if there had been one, had faltered on his arrival and he was beginning to feel a wee bit awkward. What can you say to somebody who has sold millions of records and whose face is recognised around the world, to somebody whose music you didn't especially like?

'Amy's off on a world tour tomorrow,' said Alison. Amy? Ye're far ben, thought Dougie.

'Yeah, I won't be back til the autumn,' said Amethyst. She had a soft voice. That seemed right for a small woman with short hair and an elf-like face but it didn't match the image of loud rock and a song being belted through a microphone.

'Ee like it here?' said Dougie at last.

'Oh yeah, it's so peaceful and so . . . so wild, if you know what I mean. The hill and the sea, everything.'

*   *   *

'It's not far, though far enough on this blasted apparatus.' Gillian, Lady Roster, was making good speed on her Zimmer over the uneven grassy path along the shore. Alecker Munro and the photographer tagged along behind her. 'Have you heard of Saint Erik?'

This question was fired at the photographer but, as he had at that moment stumbled into a rabbit hole, he didn't answer. Lady Roster didn't seem to notice and carried on talking.

'Interesting guy for a holy man. He slaughtered a few dozen Celts and had his wicked way with their women and then became a Christian. Went around healing the sick, curing the blind and the deaf. All legend of course, but there must be some truth behind it. Died on a fishbone. Ah, here we are.'

The three stopped and surveyed their destination. In the brae they saw the Holy Well of the saint. The ground below the spring was bright green and speckled with marsh marigolds. It looked spongy.

Alecker suggested that he and Lady Roster should stand above the well for the photograph. The two of them made their way around the boggy bit as best they could but the legs of the Zimmer sank threateningly and brown water gurgled up around them.

'Blast, I think I'm stuck,' cried Lady Roster. 'I know, you'll have to carry me.'

'Eh?'

'Carry me. Are you deaf as well? You'd better drink some of the water, see if it cures you. Turn around and stand here. Closer. Remember piggy backs?'

Alecker found Lady Roster's arms clamping tightly around his neck and forcing him to bend down. 'Take my legs,' she ordered. He reluctantly reached for her thighs and his hands brushed nervously over thick stocking material and bloomers. She was some weight but he managed to lever her up and staggered with his burden on to drier ground, to the noise of a camera shutter clicking furiously.

Alecker straightened and glared at the grinning photographer.

'Right,' snapped Lady Roster. 'Where do you want us? Here?'

'That'll do nicely. Another one. Alecker, move closer to . . . closer . . . put your hand on her shoulder . . . no, maybe . . . okay . . . look at me.'

But Alecker was looking at two figures rapidly approaching across the field. He recognised one immediately as Magnus Stroup and then saw the other was Pogo the scaffieman.

'Mr Stroup,' bellowed Lady Roster, and the councillor frowned unhappily. 'You're in luck. Come and have your picture taken at the Holy Well of Saint Erik. I discovered it.'

Magnus maintained a painful silence but Pogo was distraught. 'Fit d'ye mean? It's my well. I found it.'

'Your well? Young man, this well has been here for over a thousand years. Have you never heard of Saint Erik?'

Pogo's dream of marketing water was in danger of evaporating. 'But . . . but I found it . . . and tasted it and all . . . and . . . it's got secret ingredients . . .'

'I wouldna be so sure o at,' said Magnus, pointing to the water in the shady cavity. They looked and saw that the well had had another visitor recently. A scattering of dark sheep droppings floated on the magic water. The four of them – the journalist, the elderly toff, the councillor and the scaffieman – stood for quite a while looking at the sheep droppings. The photographer clicked busily.

'I think at's sabotage,' breathed Pogo finally.

'Don't be silly,' said Lady Roster. 'It's a sheep. They have no sense of evil.'

Pogo wasn't so sure. He also wasn't sure how much he should reveal about his plan to bottle the well water and sell it as an elixir on the healthfood market.

'Well, there it is,' went on Lady Roster. 'The Holy Well of Saint Erik. I mentioned it in my brochure, which you've got and no doubt read, Mr Stroup, but I wasn't sure of its exact location at the time. Is it too late to amend the text?'

Magnus tried to keep the relief out of his voice. 'You're just in time before it goes to the press.'

The photographer called to them to regroup for a final picture.

'I think Mr Stroup should be seen sampling the waters,' suggested Lady Roster. 'Now, down you go beside the well, Mr Stroup.'

Magnus protested but there was nothing for it but to kneel beside the stone cistern and put out his hand as if it were cupped full of the health-giving water. The photographer called to him to smile as if he had just tasted some and found it good. Manfully, the councillor ignored the gutters seeping over the rim of his right shoe and forced a grin.

July

Sinclair Cattach watched with approval as Bowser Clett lifted two large crabs from the dripping cage on the deck of the *Polaris*. He nodded with satisfaction and commented that they were a good size and had definitely put on weight.

'D'ye think so?' said Bowser.

'I told you this would be promising,' said Cattach. 'I told you that crab-ranching is the way of the future and we would be pioneers.'

Bowser commented that the other crabs in the cage hadn't grown much. Cattach peered through the netting. 'They're healthy, though. Give them some more feeding and leave them another wee whilie.'

They tipped some dead cuddanes into the cage, fastened the door and pushed the contraption over the side of the boat. It splashed and sank from sight, under a twisting pillar of silvery bubbles.

'I dinna see any sign o Wildy,' said Bowser, after he had scanned the empty sea around them. He went to the wheelhouse and put the engine into gear. The *Polaris* surged and danced through the waves.

As they came through the jaws of the harbour entrance, Cattach turned to Bowser and shouted 'Himself is home again. See, on the quay!'

'Fa?' Bowser looked and saw a tall young man in a long coat. The coat was odd in itself on such a bright day but the appearance of the waiting man was made stranger by the fact his hair was bright scarlet. There was no mistaking Mark Milton.

'I think I raithered the blue,' mused Cattach.

'He looks like a parrot,' growled Bowser, slipping the clutch as the boat slid towards the quayside.

'Aye, Mark,' shouted Cattach, throwing him a rope. 'Ye're home again. Just slip that bicht ower the bollard ere like a good loon.'

Mark hopped agilely aboard as soon as the *Polaris* was made fast. 'Good catch,' he observed and, seeing the quizzical look on Cattach's face, added that he was no longer a vegetarian but had become a piscivore.

'A pissy fit?' escaped from Bowser.

'I eat seafood.'

Bowser grunted, as if to signify satisfaction for at least one sign of normality in the chiel. Then it occurred to him that maybe he was seeking a boil of crabs.

'Now, this is just grand,' cried Cattach. 'Here you are home. The forecast is good for the next few days, and Bowser and me have time on our hands. I think it's time we made a trippie.'

'Trippie?' cried Bowser.

'Stroma. How about e morn?'

'I'm game,' said Mark.

'Come on, Bowser, ee canna say no. Ye're outvoted two til one.'

Bowser glowered and found it necessary to check the knots on the mooring ropes. Mark watched him and whispered to Cattach, who was now leaning on the winch with a nonchalent air, that maybe it wasn't such a good idea. Cattach smiled and shook his head. Bowser disappeared below the wheelhouse and for a few seconds they heard nothing but mysterious gurgles and then bilgewater began to spew from the *Polaris*.

'All richt then,' muttered the skipper when he eventually rose into view again. 'We'll have til catch e ebb. At'll be an early start. And I want a fiver fae each o ee for diesel.'

'If you insist on putting a monetary value on a scientific investigation . . .' began Cattach, but Mark interrupted him and said it was a deal, and that was that.

'Well, I'll see you boys tomorrow morning,' cried the minister's son in delight. 'Stroma here we come.'

When Mark had departed, Bowser muttered that he didn't understand this keenness to get to Stroma.

'Atlantis,' said Cattach. 'We're both of a scientific bent. Where's your natural curiosity?'

*　　*　　*

Miss Sarah Job made her way along the village street to the shop, not thinking about very much. She paid no attention to a large, gleaming car parked outside the door, and went in. Jean was leaning on the counter and smiling at a man in a smart jacket. Sarah saw that this stranger had a straight, sharp crease down the backs of his trouser legs and that his shoes were polished to a high shine. Her brain remembered the car and automatically connected the two. What really made her pause, however, was the smile on Jean's face.

'No, I've never been til Spain,' she was saying. When she noticed Sarah she stopped smiling and resumed her usual frown. 'What can I do for ee?'

'Weel . . .' began Sarah, absently. 'I've run out o Whiskas and I was . . .'

'The pet food's ower ere,' said Jean brusquely.

'Spain is marvellous.' This was the stranger talking. 'Sun, the sand, the Sangria, the nightlife . . .'

'Ower ere,' snapped Jean, and then she spoke to the man again, 'Sorry, well, I widna know about nightlife or San-what-you-said. It's a long way fae Brimster.'

'Just a mere plane flight,' said the stranger with a cheery laugh. 'A couple of hours in the sky and there you are.'

Jean laughed. She actually laughed, and to Sarah it was such an unusual sound that it spurred her to snatch two tins of Whiskas and step smartly up the counter. 'I was in London myself,' she said.

'Well, that doesn't surprise me,' said the stranger, turning to her. Sarah noticed the carnation in his buttonhole and the fact that he was shorter than either herself or Jean. He also had his hair well groomed. 'You look like a lady of the world.'

No one had ever called Sarah a lady of the world before and she wasn't sure exactly how desirable this was, but Jean didn't give her long to think about it and quickly asked for the payment. 'Is there anything else?' she asked, as she handed the change to Sarah.

'Weel . . . eh . . . no,' replied Sarah firmly. 'That's quite enough for now.' And she took the tins of cat food and left. When the door closed behind her, though, she stayed on the pavement and gave the car a once-over. On the back seat stood a box with samples of merchandise and a thick folder of papers. There were some more papers on the front passenger seat. Sarah peered cautiously at them. She couldn't see very much without her reading glasses but, by moving her head back and fore, she was able to bring into focus a letter. It was addressed to a Mr C. Clove.

'Hm-hm,' said Sarah in a tone of satisfaction.

*   *   *

'Ah well, it was a good idea but I dinna think it would have worked.' Magnus Stroup was trying to console Pogo, whose dream of bottling water from the well by the shore and selling it as an elixir had just been shattered.

'We could clean oot e sheep's dirt and fence it off.'

'No,' said Magnus. 'I think Lady Roster's right. The best thing til do is til publicise it as e Holy Well o Saint Erik in e tourist brochure and leave it at at. Besides, e market for bottled mineral waters is saturated. There's a few firms at have sunk in bottled water.'

Pogo didn't want to give up so easily. 'But it's a holy well, so fit if it was able til work miracles?'

'There hasna been a miracle in Brimster since . . .' began Magnus, and then corrected himself, 'I suspect there's never been a miracle in Brimster full stop and I think ye're wastan your time til think along at lines.'

*   *   *

Early morning at Brimster harbour. Mark, still with his hair dyed scarlet, was on the quay ready and packed for the voyage when Cattach came ambling down the steps. 'Ah well, you're on time,' observed the old man. 'Now all we need is the ancient mariner.'

No sooner had he spoken than Bowser's bulky silhouette hove into view on the braehead. 'The captain's always last aboard,' said Cattach.

'Weel, I hope ee ken fit ye're goan for,' cried Bowser as he reached the *Polaris* and surveyed the other two, waiting on the deck.

'I told you already,' said Cattach sonorously. 'Atlantis.'

'A lot o nonsense,' was Bowser's only comment as he disappeared into the wheelhouse to start the engine.

'He has no curiosity,' said Cattach sorrowfully to Mark. 'Never had any.'

'Do you seriously think Atlantis is linked with Stroma?' asked Mark.

Cattach frowned. 'Well, I dinna ken but if you look on the internet you'll find a lot of people who are lookan for it. Some says it's in e South China Sea, ithers say Antarctica, Crete, South America. I see no reason til rule oot e possibility o Stroma. Besides, at's only for Bowser's benefit.' And he winked.

Mark smiled. 'You still haven't told him about Wildy.'

'No, it's best he disna ken. Efter all, Wildy approached us in confidence about his grandfaither's treasure and a man must keep his word. Husht now.'

The engine spluttered and fired, and Bowser's head emerged from the wheelhouse. 'Cast off!'

'Here we go,' cried Mark. 'I'm looking forward to this.'

The *Polaris* punched her way out from the harbour and, after clearing the skerries, Bowser turned her head in the direction of the Firth and Stroma. A haze obscured the horizon and a long slow swell moved across the sea but otherwise it was a good day for a cruise. As they moved along the coast, Mark brought out a pair of binoculars and scanned the rocks, looking for birds and seals.

'Ye'll have heard about the silkie legends,' said Cattach. 'At they can take on human form and walk on the land. I'm no sure there's anything in at myself.'

'You mean you might believe it?' said Mark in surprise.

'No, but I keep an open mind,' replied Cattach.

*   *   *

Miss Sarah Job's mind was turning over the idea that Jean in the shop just had to be up to something. This bothered Sarah and she

said as much to her cat: 'Yes, Smokey, she was all laughing and joking with this stranger, a Mr Clove, and she was very sharp and obviously did not want me to be around.' Smokey had no opinion on the shopkeeper's odd behaviour. Sarah concluded that she needed to carry out more field work.

The bell on the shop door tinkled a little too loudly for Sarah's liking as, some fifteen minutes later, she went in with all her senses on full alert. Jean was studying a book but she closed it and slid it beneath some newspapers when she saw the old spinster.

'Well,' said Jean. 'Better day.'

'Weel . . . aye, maybe,' said Sarah quietly. 'I need two tins o Whiskas.'

'Ye had two tins yesterday,' said Jean suddenly.

Of course, this was true. Cat food had been the very thing she had come to buy when she had caught – this was the right word for it – caught Jean and her Mr Clove the day before. Sarah gave herself a black mark but, if she had betrayed herself, it was too late to back out now and she muttered hastily that Smokey had a big appetite.

'Is at e only kind at'll do?' asked Jean. 'There's none left on e shelf. I'll have til open a new case.'

Sarah inwardly thanked Providence for this stroke of fortune. 'Oh aye, he's awful fussy, he'll no eat anything else.'

'Ye spoil at cats o yours,' grumbled Jean, and she went off to the store to find the stock.

As if with a will of their own, Sarah's fingers inched towards the book under the newspapers but Jean returned before they reached their destination and they quickly withdrew as the shopkeeper thumped two tins on the counter. Sarah was not to be outdone, however, and taking a deep breath she announced that she would take a paper as well and had her hand out pulling at them before Jean could say another word. Somehow the hidden book slipped into view.

'Oh, weel, are ee learning Spanish?' asked Sarah loudly when she saw the cover.

'At's an order,' snapped Jean, but Sarah noted with satisfaction that the shopkeeper's face had turned a deeper shade of red and merely commented 'Oh weel' as she rummaged through her purse.

*   *   *

Bowser Clett watched his two passengers as the *Polaris* made her way Stroma-wards. The fisherman still couldn't fathom why the minister's son had to keep dying his hair different colours. Still he had to admit that in every other way Mark seemed a nice enough chiel. Too muckle brains, thought Bowser, maybe that's it, makes folk act in a funny way, maybe like a tank of water that's overfilled, the excess has to spill out somehow. Cattach was just as bad, though he hadn't taken yet to dying his hair, which was just as well at his age. The old chiel was full of daft ideas and seemed in no way embarrassed to air them.

'I think ee should use a false name next time ee write a letter til e *Groat*,' Bowser had once observed, after Cattach had sent in a long missive on how by mixing porpoise and human DNA it might be possible to clone a mermaid.

'A man should never be ashamed o his honest opinion,' had been Cattach's response.

Now what was Cattach doing? He had unfolded a large sheet of paper and was bending over it with a small chain in his hand. As Bowser watched, his friend moved the gently swinging chain slowly over the paper.

'I dinna like ee doan at,' shouted Bowser. 'We're at e sea.'

'Don't fash,' was Cattach's reply. 'You've always been a superstitious man. There is no record o divining bringing bad luck til mariners.'

Bowser girned. 'Any response?' asked Mark.

'I'm not gettan a reading at all,' said Cattach. 'Maybe the motion o the boat is interfering wi the energy lines.'

Mark resumed his scanning of the ocean and the coast. 'There's another boat over there,' he said.

Bowser peered across the sea. 'Looks like Wildy,' he announced. 'Fit's he doan yonder? He hasna any creels on at ground.'

This seemed to alarm Cattach. He sat up, took the binoculars from Mark and focused on the distant craft. 'It is the *Girl Ina*. He's on the same course.'

'I micht have kent it,' cried Bowser. 'He's followan us. Fit would he be doan at for? Gies a look wi at gless.' The view through the binoculars confirmed the fisherman's suspicion. 'Aye, he's followan us richt enough. I dinna ken fit he's up til, but I'm goan til find oot.' He turned the wheel to send the *Polaris* into a wide arc on the sea. Mark staggered as the waves made the boat rock.

Cattach caught his arm to steady him. 'Do you think we should tell him about Wildy?' whispered Mark.

For once Cattach seemed caught with no answer. Eventually, as the boat settled on her new course, he muttered that it would maybe be better to say nothing in the meantime. 'Are you sure?' Cattach nodded and had to grab for support himself when Bowser opened the throttle and gunned the *Polaris* across the sea.

'He seems pretty mad,' said Mark, glancing aft at the skipper's grim visage, now with the bonnet rammed down hard over the eyes.

'Like a plucker,' agreed Cattach. 'I think the game's up but I gave my word to Wildy that I would tell nobody about Owld Toftie's treasure. It's always best never til surrender the moral high ground, Mark. I'm sure your faither, being the minister, would agree.'

The two boats approached each other. Bowser started to bellow across the intervening space and scared two scarfs into flight.

'We don't have VHF,' said Cattach to Mark. 'Til tell the truth, Bowser doesna need it when his dander's up.'

'Wildy Ham,' roared the irate fisherman. 'I ken fit ye're up til and dinna say different. Ye're efter my crab ranch. I would never have put ee doon for a . . . a . . . crab rustler, Wildy.'

They could see Wildy standing beside his wheelhouse. He seemed to be alone and, as they neared each other, he began to shout back. The words were disjointed at first and Mark put up a quick prayer that, for the sake of peace, Bowser's accusation had been equally jumbled in transmission.

'. . . wastan . . . time . . . tellt ee . . . shark's teeth . . . jumbo . . .'

Cattach went aft just before Bowser could let loose another broadside of invective. 'It's no the crabs he's after.'

'Fit ither is it, then?' exploded Bowser.

'Treasure!'

'Treasure?' Bowser stared at Cattach and pushed up his bonnet, an act that seemed to relieve his temper along with the pressure on his brow.

'Aye,' said Cattach, and he now raised his voice, throwing the words across the narrowing gap between the boats. 'Wildy, ahoy. What news?'

'I thocht it was Atlantis ee was lookan for,' protested Bowser.

Wildy's voice came to them. 'It was all a carry-on for nothing. I knew it. Hing on.'

The boats turned on to parallel courses and, throttles eased, they sailed along together to allow a conversation at a more reasonable volume.

'I kent fit ee were on,' cried Wildy. 'Makan for Stroma til look for Owld Toftie's treasure. I'm no pleased ee went withoot me and I wish I'd left ee til it, and no chase efter ee til tell ee ye're wastan your time.'

'Na, na, Wildy, we wouldna do such a thing,' shouted Cattach. 'It's Atlantis.'

'Aye, weel, we got a letter. Fae e solicitor. It was all a hoax by e owld chiel.'

'Fit owld chiel?' demanded Bowser.

'Owld Toftie,' said Cattach, 'I'll tell ee later.'

Wildy was shouting again. 'Toftie was gettan his own back on his dochters for always gettan on at him aboot money. He planned e whole thing for revenge.'

'I must say I'm disappointed,' cried Mark.

'I'm no,' replied Wildy. 'I kent all along. I telt ee yon mumbo-jumbo wi a shark's teeth was no use. Weel, I'm goan til try some flies for bait.'

As the *Girl Ina* began to turn away, Cattach told the now-mystified Bowser how Owld Toftie had left a cryptic message that they thought referred to a fortune hidden on Stroma. 'We thocht we micht have a lookie for it at e same time as we did our scientific investigations for Atlantis,' concluded Cattach, 'but it seems now it was all a hoax.'

'And fit was all at aboot shark's teeth?' asked Bowser.

'Well, I did a bit o divining,' muttered Cattach a little lamely, 'but it didna work very good. Even famous scientists have made the odd mistake.'

Bowser opened the throttle a bit. 'Weel, are we still on for Stroma or no?' he asked.

'It's a good day,' commented Cattach quietly.

The *Polaris* resumed her course and Cattach went for'ad to join Mark.

'Look there,' cried the minister's son. 'Looks like a yacht.'

'Oh aye, we get a few o them in the summer.'

Mark focused the binoculars on the craft. 'The sail seems all loose,' he announced. 'Can't quite make out the flag on the stern.'

Suddenly, as they watched, a trail of smoke shot up from the yacht, hung for a moment in the air and then exploded into a coloured star. The crack of an explosion reached their ears.

'Good heavens, he's in distress,' cried Cattach.

Bowser had also seen the flare. He stuck his head from the wheelhouse, shouted that they had better see what was up and altered course towards the distant yacht. As she came nearer, the men could see that the vessel's sail was piled uselessly on the roof of the superstructure and that she was beginning to wallow.

'He's lost all his way,' commented Cattach. 'Gies look with the gless.' Mark handed over the binoculars and the old man focused on the stricken craft. 'Well I never,' he breathed, 'I know that flag on the stern. She's Faroese.'

*   *   *

Back ashore, in Brimster, Pogo was wrestling with a difficulty at the same time as he was wrestling with the wheelie bins. But fa was iss chiel Saint Erik, Pogo asked himself, I wonder fit he looked like.

Images of holy men had not figured strongly in Pogo's education but he gradually formed a vague notion of someone tall, dressed in a long robe, with a long white beard, carrying a stick.

'Hurry up wi at bin.' Lang Tam was leaning from the cab. 'Are ee goan til stand e whole day dreaman?'

Dreep pushed the empty bin back to the roadside. Pogo glanced at them both and asked himself how they might react if they came suddenly face to face with Saint Erik.

*   *   *

Several people had noticed that the character of Jean in the shop had shown a sudden change. She had become less ill-natured, she spoke to customers cheerily, even ventured a joke. This metamorphosis took everyone so much by surprise that they commented on it to each other, though usually in hushed tones, in case the unwise mention of it might cause a reversal to the old regime.

'Jean's awful happy iss days,' said Magnus Stroup to his wife. 'She even smiled at me. Has she come up in e Lottery?'

'I don't know,' said Peggy Stroup. 'If she's become rich, we should soon see.'

'Jean couldn't have been nicer to me today. She even played with Emma,' Alison told Dougie.

Miss Sarah Job, however, knew exactly what was going on and told her cat. 'The limmer's in love, Smokey. She's carrying on wi Mr Clove the traveller, and learning Spanish. They're going til elope til Torremolinos and lie on the beach in the sun. Brimster's no good enough for her any more.'

* * *

Meanwhile the *Polaris* had reached the yacht. She was indeed a Faroese vessel, the *Sula*, and she needed help. There were three people aboard – a young man who introduced himself to the rescuers as Peter, his wife Liv, and another young woman called Kirsten. They had run into some rough weather on their voyage from the Faroes and sea water had contaminated their fuel; as if that were not bad enough, the weakened mast had threatened to give way and they had been forced to take in sail to ease the strain on it.

'Never mind, you're all right now,' Cattach reassured them. 'We'll give you a tow til Brimster and you can lie up to make your repairs.'

Now Bowser was steering the *Polaris* for home and the *Sula* was dancing in her wake, the tow rope stretching and dipping.

'I was in the Faroes, you know,' Cattach was telling Mark. 'In the war. I was in the Royal Navy and we used to dodge in and out o Thorshaven. I got on well there. Faroese is a bit like the way we speak here, you know.'

Bowser overheard this. 'Fan ee tried it on them,' he said, nodding in the direction of the yacht, 'they couldna make oot a word ee was sayan.'

'Ah well, maybe my pronunciation has gone a bit roosty through lack o practice,' admitted Cattach. 'It was a while ago and I was a young man then.'

Wildy Ham was fishing not far away and Bowser took the *Polaris* over by him, and shouted across the water about what had happened. Wildy waved and cried he would catch up with them later. After another half an hour, the fishing boat and the yacht reached the harbour. Bowser pointed to where the *Sula* could tie up and took the *Polaris* to her own berth. When all was secure and moored, the mariners met on the quay.

Peter thanked them and they told him to think nothing of it. 'Mind you, a pint wouldna go far wrong,' said Cattach, and he and the three Faroese set off along the quay. Bowser watched them.

'Something wrong?' asked Mark when he saw the keen expression on the skipper's face.

'No,' said Bowser. 'Nothing's wrong, but I just thocht something at I would hardly have believed if it wasna for ma own een at saw it.'

*   *   *

'This is very nice,' said Peter, the Faroese skipper, in his careful English. 'Lunch in a Scottish pub. What is this?'

'At's neeps,' said Bowser helpfully. 'Mince and tatties, wi neeps. Just e stuff ee need.'

The rescued and the rescuers made a merry little party. Peter's wife, Liv, tasted the mince and pronounced it good; and the third member of the yacht's crew, Kirsten, said she admired Mark's scarlet hair. 'I'm thinking of trying another colour,' said the minister's son, and Bowser shot a worried glance at him. It seemed he'd been through the rainbow already.

Margaret the landlady and Cattach came over with laden trays and distributed the drinks. Cattach raised his whisky and toasted the visitors' arrival. 'Thank you, thank you,' cried Peter. 'You will not be angry if I say we hope it will not be long.'

'Ye'll need a day or two til sort the engine,' said Cattach. 'I dinna ken about the mast. It might be hard til get the bits.'

'We have stores aboard,' explained Peter. 'We need perhaps time to fix.'

As it happened Cattach was sitting beside Kirsten. The young woman was tall and had long, brownish hair. Liv, on the other hand, was quite short and had cropped blonde hair. Both concentrated on their food while Cattach quizzed Peter about their voyage and their intentions, and Bowser, who was shortly to go down the street for his own dinner at home, watched them all closely as he sipped his stout.

A few other customers came and went. Dougie appeared, bringing the whiff of the byre with him, and had a pint. Two tourists sat over salad rolls and lager. Karen Toft and Susan Ham came to the side door to buy crisps. Karen's father, Ian Toft, celebrated cutting the grass in his garden by buying himself a pint of heavy, and John Campbell came in, in his overalls, time out from the garage.

'At's e man ee want,' said Bowser.

John eased his rotund bulk between the tables and grinned at the mention of his name. The bald head, the flying tufts of hair above his lugs and the overalls smeared with grease gave him the appearance of a down-at-heel monk.

'He is engineer?' asked Peter.

'Weel, I'll hev a go but I'm no promisan anything.' This was John's second most common response, the first being 'Take her in and we'll hev a lookie.'

John nodded and grinned as the situation was explained, and he said he would come down in the afternoon to examine the engine.

The next person to come through the door made all the natives of Brimster pause, look at each other and transmit an unspoken question. What had brought Miss Sarah Job into the profane environs of the Arms? Was it an illusion? Well, there she was, a little hesitant perhaps, a bit unsure of herself in this strange place, but definitely there, because she spoke.

'Oh weel . . . hello,' she said. 'I was looking for . . .' And as she said these words, her eyes shuttled around everyone present. 'But . . . oh, it's yourself, Margaret,' and with that she went up to the bar and spoke in a low voice that defeated the straining ears of the others.

'Yes,' said Margaret more loudly, to everyone's gratification. 'That man was in a whilie ago but he's no here now.'

'Oh weel,' said Sarah. 'Eh . . . excuse me. Hello, Dougie, John, Ian, Sinclair . . . eh . . . I'd better be going then,' and she edged her way out again, and the door closed behind her. Outside in the hotel carpark, her face hardened. Yes, the car was there, it was his car all right, there was no mistaking the large, shining automobile. But the driver was not in the bar and, to Sarah, this meant he could only be in one other place. She glared across the road in the direction of the shop, where a 'closed for lunch' sign hung in the door, and debated what to do.

Back in the Brimster Arms, Bowser realised he should have been home long ago but, despite the flyting he would get from his wife, he could not bring himself to abandon the party. Cattach had begun to tell of his own visits to the Faroes.

'Aye, we used til dodge in and out of Thorshaven all the time. On patrol, you ken. And we went all over. I was in Klaksvik and Vestmanna and all the fjords. Wild weather sometimes but lovely islands.'

'You were in Klaksvik?' cried Kirsten. 'I am from Klaksvik.'

'Fancy at,' said Cattach. 'We used til go til dances in Klaksvik.'

The conversation buzzed around life in Klaksvik, the fishing town in the north of the Faroes, and Kirsten took some photographs and postcards from her pocket to show what the place looked like. Cattach nodded his recognition of this street and that kirk. Among the pictures were photos of people. Bowser, his wife's cutting tongue and burnt dinner forgotten, peered closely at them.

'That is my grandmother,' said Kirsten. 'She is now dead. That is my mother and father. My grandfather. My other grand-father is not here.'

Bowser said 'Oh aye' in a noncommittal way and eased back on his chair. He no longer had any doubt. It all fitted – the dates, the photos, and now the clincher was right here in front of him, in the astonishing resemblance between these two people. Kirsten was no other than Cattach's own granddaughter.

'I don't believe it,' said Isobel Clett when her errant husband had at last turned up for his dinner and told her his news. The revelation had quite taken the steam out of the flyting she was ready to give him. 'Cattach's an owld bachelor.'

'Ah, but he was a young bachelor once,' said Bowser, tucking into his well-fired steak pie.

'All e same, I've never heard tell o him wi a wife, even during e war.'

'Fa's talkan aboot a wife?'

Isobel nodded as she turned over this piece of news and finally asked what Cattach himself had said.

'Oh nothing,' said Bowser cheerfully. 'He doesna ken yet, but they are as like ain anither as twa peas. She's called Kirsten and her age would fit wi fan he was in e Faroes. Fancy us being e ones til rescue them.'

'Are ee goan til tell him?'

'No, I dinna think I could do at. We'll wait and see if he catches on.'

*　　*　　*

Miss Sarah Job had never seen herself as a secret agent but she was making a good go of it, lurking in the willows and geiks where she had a clear view of the shop. Every so often she whispered loudly 'Puss, puss' and moved around but, as her cat was curled up asleep on her own couch, this was merely a stratagem to fool passers-by. She kept this up for about five minutes and then realised that the patch of overgrown ground was too small to warrant further supposed searching and that she had better think of something else to pretend to do. Fortunately the bus shelter outside the hotel had a couple of posters on it and she decided they were crying out for careful reading.

She had almost memorised the bus timetable and the names of the players in the next Brimster Rangers game by the time her clandestine mission achieved success. First, however, she was almost thwarted by the arrival of the bus. As it stopped, the hiss of the brakes and the automatic door took her by surprise and she gaped blindly at the driver.

'Well, are ee gettan on?' he asked brusquely.

At that moment Sarah glimpsed a movement at the shop door. Suddenly everything was happening at once and, flustered, she stammered 'Weel . . . eh . . . no . . . sorry' to the disgruntled driver, and then disgruntled him further by diving across the road in front of his vehicle.

When she reached the other side and the beat in her heart had eased a little, Sarah sidled along the wall.

'Eh . . . weel, hello,' she said, and she knew that she was blushing.

Mr Clove, commercial traveller, had just eaten a copious lunch at Jean's table and smiled benignly at the little old woman he had flattered by saying she was a lady of the world. He had forgotten saying it, but Sarah hadn't.

'I was just wondering, Mr Clove,' went on the emboldened Sarah. After all, this was how she thought ladies of the world ought to behave. 'That perhaps you might care til drop in for . . . a cuppie o tea some time.'

Mr Clove smiled and smoothed his silk tie. 'I must say that's very nice of you. I'm afraid I'm tied up this afternoon.' Sarah's face registered disappointment but brightened again when he added, 'Would this day next week be convenient?'

'It would be perfect,' agreed Sarah and she made sure he had her address by handing him a piece of paper where it was already written. 'Weel, at's fine then,' she smiled, 'I'll be seeing ee . . . later.' As he went across the road to his car, she stopped herself from calling out after him that she hoped he liked cats.

* * *

John Campbell and Peter were almost out of sight, squeezed down in the narrow space beside the *Sula*'s engine. The mechanic had come to the harbour, as he had promised, and was examining the fuel system. Peter thought sea water had contaminated the diesel. Cattach sat on the coaming and listened to their conversation, from time to time throwing down a suggestion.

Bowser ambled down the quay. 'Far's e weemen?' he asked.

'They are having a walk til themsels along e shore,' announced Cattach. 'Mark is taking them on a guided tour.'

Bowser grunted and sat on a fish box. He felt sorely tempted to reveal what he had concluded about Kirsten but, looking at Cattach's thin frame curled over the superstructure of the boat, he wondered if the shock might not be too much. Surely he'll twig, thought Bowser, though he can be a thrawn owld bugger fan he wants til, and I micht just have til shoogle him along a bit.

'I've invited Peter and the ladies til join me for their tea,' announced Cattach suddenly.

'In e hotel?'

'No, I'm going til cook for them myself. It's a way o saying thank you til their country for their kindness til a homesick sailor during e dark days o e war.'

Bowser could think of nothing to say.

* * *

Meanwhile Pogo had reached a conclusion. It would have to be tomorrow morning – it was the best time in the week, in fact the only time his plan would work, as tomorrow he and his fellow scaffies would be doing the village and what Pogo had in mind had to take place in the village. To be more specific, it had to happen at the harbour, and that was the binmen's first stop.

*   *   *

A thick bank of sea fog lay over Brimster harbour and visibility was reduced to only a few yards at the early hour at which the garbage truck rolled to a stop beside the wheelie bin on the quay. Dreep jumped down from the cab.

'I wonder what's happened til Pogo?' Dreep had said. 'D'ye think he's no weel? Should we go til see?'

Lang Tam would have none of this. If Pogo failed to turn up, it was his problem and Dreep would have to manage without his companion as best he could. Tam's big head hung out from the driver's window as he watched Dreep free the bin. Just then, Dreep stopped and looked up.

'Did ee hear at?' he asked.

Tam glanced left and right in the fog. He had heard a noise, a low rising moan it had been, but where it had come from neither of them could tell. Then they heard it again, and this time it sounded closer.

Dreep started back in surprise. A figure had risen from among the old creels and fish boxes heaped behind the bin. It was a tall shape, draped in white, and a long white beard flowed from the half-hidden face. The left hand of this strange apparition held a long staff but the right hand was pointing at Dreep.

'Are ee a ghost?' stammered the binman.

'I am Saint Erik the Holy,' intoned the figure in a sonorous, yet young-sounding voice. 'I command ee, Dreep, and ee, Lang Tam, til spread e word at ee've seen me and pass on my message til Councillor Stroup and e newspapers. If ee do iss, I'll make e rich. Iss is an offer ee canna refuse.'

Dreep recovered enough of his poise to turn to Lang Tam. 'Hey, at sounds lek e Mafia.'

Lang Tam, whose eyes were popping from his head, misheard the question. 'Fit's at? E Scaffia?'

'Well, maybe, ye're richt,' cried Dreep, and he addressed the holy ghost. 'Pogo, if at's ee, ee can come oot o at sheet now.'

*   *   *

Dougie sat at his computer and punched at the keys. Emma was crawling on a mat on the kitchen floor and gurgling happily, as her father waited for any emails to download. 'We've got one,' he announced to his daughter. 'Fit does it say?' Emma gurgled some more.

'Hey,' cried Dougie suddenly. 'Some chiel wants til buy tatties and some cabbage. It works. At's wir first sale ower e internet. Alison!'

His wife came from the kitchen where she had been washing dishes. 'We've got an order. Is at no great?' Alison, who had been dealing with pottery stores for a long time, smiled at her husband's excitement. 'It's the age o the electronic crofter,' he chortled.

'Talking of electronics, the video man is coming to shoot the lambs for the mart.'

'Oh aye. We're goan til be on a video, Emma. How does at appeal til ee?'

Emma rolled around on her mat and gurgled some more.

*   *   *

'Ee gave us a fricht,' admitted Dreep, 'but no for long. No ghost would sound lek at. They would speak polite. Fit was ee up til?'

Pogo sat disconsolately in the cab of the garbage truck, the white sheet he had worn bundled in his lap. The beard and wig he had made from pieces of old rope lay on top. 'I'm no sayan anything. It didna work, at's all.'

'Of course, it didna work,' growled Lang Tam. 'A richt carry on. No chiel believes in ghosts and saints now. Iss is e new Millennium.'

'I thocht I was on til something wi e watter fae e holy well but no chiel took me seriously,' complained Pogo. 'I thocht maybe a ghost would shake folk up and make them think again. At's anither chance til make some money gone west. Is there no way til get rich in Brimster?'

Dreep thought for a moment before saying quietly, 'Just because we recognised ee doesna mean everybody else would. The question is which person wouldna be so quick on e uptake.'

'It's Magnus we have til convince. If he's for it, it'll be a goer.'

'Name one person in Brimster at Magnus is frichtened o,' said Dreep. 'Ye're lookan blank. I'll tell ee. Lady Roster.'

Pogo's face took on a look of terror. 'No her. I'm no appearan til her as e ghost o Saint Erik.'

'It's perfect,' argued Dreep. 'She's e perfect target. If she believes in ee, she'll tell Magnus and he'll no dare go against her.'

'Are ee gettan at bins e day or e morn?' shouted Tam, as he braked the truck at the end of the village street.

'Can ee no see e soundness o e plan?' said Dreep as they got down from the cab. 'I'll come wi ee. E only question is – when is e best time til do it?'

*   *   *

Dougie had combed his hair and put on a clean shirt in time for the arrival of the two men with the video camera, as if he were to be filmed and not the lambs he had to sell. Alison, with Emma in her arms, came out to watch the proceedings. They all went to the park where Dougie had corralled the animals earlier. Annabella the goat followed them.

'We've just come fae Short Bob's,' said the video man. 'At took longer than expected. Bob kept gettan intil the shot. He would insist on steeran aboot among e lambs. I felt like tying him til a stab until we were done.'

'Bob has always had a secret fancy til be a film star,' said Dougie. 'E good, e bad and e ugly all rolled intil one. I've still got four o his sheep here.'

'Aye, he told us about them,' said the video man. 'We'll make a separate shot o them. Murdoch Ure at Meldale has another four o Bob's. We can edit all the shots together.'

The man with the camera prowled around and recorded images of the lambs. It started to spit with rain but the filming went on, and soon the job was done.

*　　*　　*

Behind the steering wheel of his van, Bowser Clett sat deep in thought. Cattach was ensconced in the back on a cushion.

'I must ask ee something?' said Bowser suddenly.

'Aye?' said Cattach absently.

The two Faroese women, Kirsten and Liv, had just gone into a shop. Bowser had driven them to town to buy some supplies. Back in Brimster harbour, Liv's husband, Peter, and John Campbell were completing repairs to the boat's engine.

'Hev ee noticed anything about Kirsten?'

'Well, she's a fine-looking lassie. What sort o thing have ee in mind?'

Bowser groaned inwardly. Cattach could be obtuse and even thick at times. There was nothing for it but to confront him, as the Faroese would be gone the next day and then it would be too late. 'Tell me again fan ee was in e Faroes,' he said.

Cattach repeated the dates and launched into a description of the fjords but Bowser interrupted him. 'And did Kirsten no say her mither was born in e war, and at she didna ken her grandfaither, but he micht have been a soldier? Fit if he had been a sailor?'

'Aye?'

'Do I have til spell it oot for ee? Kirsten is e spittan image o ee, except for being a wumman. Did ee no notice?'

Cattach sat up abruptly and banged his head on the van roof. He rubbed his bonnet.

'Ee telt me aboot e dances ee used til go til, and how friendly e Faroese weemen were,' went on Bowser.

'Say no more,' muttered Cattach. 'At couldna be.'

'Weel, ee ken yoursel. Unless ee've forgotten.'

'No,' murmured Cattach. 'I hevna forgotten. I just never thought. Michty me, fancy at. Efter all these years, I've got a granddochter.' Then he cried in a flustered voice. 'Does she ken?'

'I dinna think so,' said Bowser. 'But now's your chance til tell her. They're coman back.'

'Now?' There was a trace of panic in Cattach's voice. After all it wasn't every day a man came face to face with a woman who might be his granddaughter but didn't know it.

'Richt now,' declared Bowser. 'Go oot and tell her, on her own. I'll keep Liv occupied.'

The Faroese had reached the van and Bowser leaned across to open the passenger door to let Liv in. At the same time he called to Kirsten that Cattach wanted to show her something and to wait until he unfolded himself from the back of the vehicle. Cattach took his time about this, as if fear was grabbing at his jacket and holding him back.

'Did ee get fit ee wanted?' said Bowser absently as Liv settled in beside him. He wasn't listening for a reply but was staring in the rear-view mirror, watching Cattach shuffling in a shamefaced kind of way and talking. Kirsten was listening intently, a serious expression on her face, Bowser saw, but then she burst into laughter and flung her arms around the old man's neck and kissed him. Bowser saw Cattach's hand go up to prevent his bonnet falling off, and then he hugged her too.

Bowser nodded contentedly and turned to Liv. 'Well, she micht have slapped him,' he said. 'It's no every chiel at would be pleased til be related til Cattach.'

*   *   *

The sun was shining on Brimster harbour, adding to the festive atmosphere, when the *Sula* made ready for departure. Peter and Liv were aboard, at the helm and the mooring ropes, and prepared to cast off as soon as the party on the quay released the third member of the crew, Kirsten, to join them.

'She sounds all richt now,' cried John Campbell, rocking on his heels like a contented monk. The healthy noise of the yacht's engine was a kind of music to his ears. 'She sounds good,' agreed the Faroese skipper, 'Thank you.'

In the centre of the crowd stood Cattach, beaming and laughing, as much from pleasure as from the effects of the whisky he had consumed. It wasn't every week a man found he had been a grandfather for years without knowing it, and if anything was a cause for celebration that had to be it.

'So, you will visit us for Christmas,' said Kirsten for the umpteenth time.

'Oh aye,' said Cattach. 'I'll go and book my ticket as soon as I get home. And if the plane is full, Bowser'll take me on the boat.'

'Aye, maybe,' said Bowser, equally red in the face.

'We must catch the tide,' called Peter from the cockpit of the *Sula*.

Kirsten gave Cattach a hug and a kiss that quite upset the old man. 'I love you,' she cried, and Cattach sniffed and drew the back of his hand across his nose. 'They always were an emotional people, e Faroese,' he muttered to Mark Milton, as Kirsten hopped smartly across the gunwale of the *Sula*.

*   *   *

Pogo sat hunched by the kitchen table and did not protest when Dreep's sister told him to shift as she washed the floor. He fidgeted sideways in his chair.

'I've never seen ee so doon in e mooth,' said Dreep. 'Ye give up too soon.'

'I wish ee two would finish your coffee and clear oot o my road,' muttered his sister, whose name was Utsira.

The whole of Brimster knew how she had come by this unusual name. Her father had been desperate for a son and had already decided to call him Donald when the shattering news that his first-born was of the other gender was revealed to him. 'That's all richt,' he had said, 'she'll be Donaldina.' His wife, however, had refused point blank to countenance such a name for her daughter and there had been a terrible row between husband and wife, so much so that the father had gone off to get drunk and had then fallen asleep.

He had woken to hear the shipping forecast and, through his stupor, had realised the poetry in North Utsire, South Utsire. Someone joked that if had woken two minutes later the hapless infant would have been christened Dogger Bank. But Utsira she became, and then, after another two years, Dreep had been born and had become the longed-for Donald. The parents were both dead now, and Dreep and Utsira lived together.

'All right,' moaned Dreep. 'We're goan. In any case we've a private matter til discuss at's confidential and all.'

'Good,' said Utsira crisply and got on with plying her mop.

Outside in the back garden, Dreep and Pogo found seclusion in the lee of the shed. 'So,' Dreep was saying, 'it's clear at it's Lady Roster ee must convince. If she gets e bit between her teeth on iss idea, there'll be no holdan her. Magnus is feard o her. He'll do anything she tells him.'

'I'm feard o her too,' moaned Pogo. 'Can ee no do it?'

'No, it's up til ee, but I'll be richt ere behind ee, dinna worry.'

*　　*　　*

Miss Sarah Job could hardly stop fidgeting. The man sitting on the couch opposite her was the image of urbanity, with his carefully combed hair, his pressed suit, his silk tie and the carnation in his buttonhole. His manners were smooth and perfect and it all made Sarah exceedingly nervous. The teapot trembled slightly in her grip as she lifted it.

'You be mother,' said Mr Clove.

'Oh . . . weel,' giggled Sarah, as she poured. 'Do you take sugar?'

'No thanks,' said Mr Clove. 'And I bet you don't. You're sweet enough already.'

Sarah felt heat in her face. Never mind, if Jean in the shop could entertain the commercial traveller, so could she, and she was determined to prove it.

'You must spend a lot of time on the road,' said Sarah bravely. 'In your job, I mean.'

Mr Clove held his cup and saucer just so as he smiled. 'Always on the go. Yes, always on the go. It's a busy life but it has its compensations.'

'Oh weel . . .'

'I mean I get to meet so many lovely people.' This was said with such perfect timing and humour that Sarah automatically sensed she was among the lovely people. This emboldened her more, and she said that perhaps he would be looking forward to the day when he could settle down.

'I dream of it sometimes,' said Mr Clove. 'A wee cottage in the country somewhere, and no more road maps and endless hours staring through a windscreen.'

'A biscuit?' asked Sarah, holding up the plate with the chocolate digestives. 'Smokey, no. Mind your manners. You'll have to excuse him. I've never seen a pussy like him for chocolate.'

'Quite a character, eh?' smiled Mr Clove smoothly.

'Oh weel, yes,' admitted Sarah. 'Just a peedie monster. Smokey, if you don't behave I'll put you to your bed.'

Mr Clove sipped his tea. I would boot the monster out the back door, he thought, but that would just upset the old dear. He enjoyed these minor flirtations during his round of rural shops but was now beginning to wonder why he had accepted this particular invitation to have a cup of tea. The desire to be somewhere other than Sarah's couch began to grow stronger when Smokey showed no signs of being deterred by his mistress's displeasure.

'I think I'll just give him a bit,' said Mr Clove, and he took a biscuit, broke it and proffered a fragment to the cat. Smokey's teeth clenched on it with a ferocity that startled the traveller.

Sarah watched in growing alarm as Smokey crunched and swallowed the titbit and immediately began to look for more. The cat put both paws on Mr Clove's elbow and stretched up towards his head. Mr Clove was not a tall man, and Smokey was a long cat, especially with his right foreleg outstretched, and the paw easily reached as far as Mr Clove's hair.

'No, Smokey, no,' cried Sarah. 'Bad boy. Oh he's just being friendly. Stop that nonsense.'

Smokey growled and withdrew but not before his claws had snagged in Mr Clove's hair. He tugged and suddenly found himself free, but some large hairy thing was still refusing to let go of his paw, shake it as he might.

Sarah's mouth fell open and no sound beyond a feeble squeak escaped. Mr Clove looked at the hairy object for at least two seconds before he realised, perhaps because he felt a slight chill on his scalp, that the strange, amorphous beast was his own toupee. He overcame the instinctive reaction to cover his baldness with both hands and instead grabbed the errant wig. A tug of war ensued on the couch.

Mr Clove stood up quickly, hoisting his wig after him and, in the process, hoisting Smokey as well until the cat finally managed to retract his claws, fell to the ground and, with a loud miaow of protest, bolted for the safety of the kitchen. Sarah sat aghast.

'You'll have to excuse me,' muttered Mr Clove, jamming the wig on his head, first back to front and then the right way.

'Oh . . . weel,' cried Sarah at last. 'There's no need til go. Your secret's safe.'

*   *   *

'Mind,' repeated Dreep, 'Ye've got til be convincing. She kens all aboot Saint Erik.'

'I'm no doan iss,' whispered Pogo.

'Ee canna give up now,' argued Dreep. 'We've come all iss way. Iss is e climax. It'll work, ee'll see.'

The two men were standing among the thick rhododendrons in the garden of the Lodge. Although it was not very late in the evening, it was already growing dark. The air in the bushes was dank under the thick sky. This was perfect, according to Dreep, as the poor visibility would work in their favour and it would be harder to see the imperfections in Pogo's garb of white sheet and long white beard.

'How are ee goan til get her til come oot?' asked Pogo.

'Chap wi your staff on e back door,' said Dreep, 'and when ee hear her coman retreat til e edge e bushes. Ee ken fit til say? Okay?'

'Ee chap and I'll wait here. I need til psych mysel up.'

'Okay.'

Dreep gave his companion a cheerful thumbs up and tiptoed across the grass to the back door. The Lodge loomed above him. When he reached the door, he rapped as loudly as he could. Watching from the rhododendrons, Pogo saw him stand back and then rap again. Nothing happened. Pogo saw Dreep look around and pick up a sawn log from a pile by the door. With this, he hammered on the door in slow beats. Then Pogo saw a light go on and the unmistakable silhouette of Gillian, Lady Roster, on the kitchen blind making her way on her Zimmer towards the noise.

'Run,' hissed Pogo, but the dryness in his throat turned the word into a low-pitched skraach.

The door was opening and Dreep was already running. Running backwards, as it happened, but he should have turned and looked where he was going because he came against something and knocked it over, and Pogo heard an ominous buzzing. Of course. The old guy Roster kept bees and Dreep had just blundered into a hive.

The door was open now. Dreep had disappeared. The buzzing grew louder. Pogo saw Lady Roster standing in the door, and realised it was now or never. He stepped forward to the edge of the bushes, raised his staff in his left hand and pointed with the other. String from his beard caught on his lips and, blowing it away, he intoned:

'I am the spirit of Saint Erik. Go forth and tell ee have met me. Tell . . .'

'What's going on here?' Lady Roster's voice boomed across the garden. 'Spirit of Saint Erik, my backside. Come out where I can see you. You're under arrest.'

'I am the spirit of Saint Erik.'

'Balderdash,' cried Lady Roster, advancing on her Zimmer at a bewildering speed and laying her hand on the saint's shoulder. 'You're under citizen's arrest.'

'Ee canna arrest a saint,' protested Pogo, as Lady Roster's podgy fingers gripped his shoulder and dug into the white sheet he wore.

'Oh, can't I?' she cried, and with her other hand she gripped the stringy tangle of rope and pulled his head forward.

'Watch my bliddy lugs,' yelled Pogo.

'Just the kind of language I would have expected from the spirit of a long-dead Norse saint,' declared Lady Roster with some satisfaction. 'Now, stop this nonsense and tell me what you're about.'

Pogo shook his head and adjusted his beard. A buzzing sound penetrated his befuddled mind and his eyes widened in alarm. 'Bees,' he whispered.

'Never mind them,' said Lady Roster. 'My husband can tend to them. Come on, come in to the kitchen.'

Skirting as widely as possible the hive Dreep had knocked over in his flight, Pogo followed the old woman as she stepped briskly on her Zimmer towards the door. As she reached it, her husband appeared. Pogo stopped short. Old man Roster wore a nightcap like a long stocking on his head and a dressing gown, and he looked a bit like a ghost himself. His wife jerked her head towards the upset hive and he loped across the damp grass to tend to it.

Lady Roster bade Pogo sit at the end of the table and take off the ridiculous mop on his chin. The light from the dim bulb in the ceiling hardly penetrated to the corners of the cavernous room but Pogo surreptitiously took in his surroundings as best he could. His gaze fell on two television sets, one perched on the other at a slight angle but so wedged about with letters and papers that it was in no risk of falling over. This strange sight hypnotized him.

Lady Roster put a glass of whisky on the table. 'Even a saint needs refreshment,' she boomed. 'Cheers.' And she plumped down at the other end with a tumbler of gin in her hand.

After Pogo had mumbled his way through an explanation of why he had been lurking in the rhododendrons dressed as a long-dead holy man, Lady Roster cackled with laughter. 'Jolly good wheeze. Wish I'd thought of that.'

Then they began to get along famously and talked over all kinds of things, including family history. It turned out that Lady Roster had known Pogo's father well, and this induced him to say that the old man had sworn to him they were descended from the house of the Stewart kings, though not exactly on the more desirable side of the blanket. Lady Roster poured herself another gin and her guest another whisky, and declared that she knew she was descended from the Picts.

'There you are,' she cried. 'We are both of the ancient Celtic races of Scotland. Not like these incomers, the Norse. Who do they think they are, what? With their Rognvalds and their Saint Eriks and their Magnuses.'

'It was Magnus I was tryan til convince,' said Pogo mournfully.

'Now, he's of Norse blood,' said Lady Roster. 'He's one of the incomers. Do you know what Stroup means?'

'No.'

'Neither do I but I'm sure it's something derogatory. Probably a sarcastic reference to his manhood. Shall we tackle Magnus?'

'Eh?'

'You and I, Pogo. We'll beard the incomer in his den. We Picts can't let some jumped-up Norseman tell us what's what, eh?'

*　　*　　*

Quite early in the morning, Miss Sarah Job put on her coat and a plastic headscarf in case it would rain and set off with a determined expression towards the village shop. Her courage carried her boldly through the door and perhaps a little of it affected the bell, for it rang with an unusually ominous tone that made Jean look up from behind the counter in surprise.

'Oh weel, now,' said Sarah. 'Is it just oursels at's in? What I have til say is strictly private.'

Jean frowned. 'Well, ee'd better get it off your chest for some chiel could come in any minute.'

'Right.' Sarah breathed in and drew herself up. 'I don't think you should think about Mr Clove again. He's a deceitful man.' She held her hand up and Jean stopped still, her mouth open, no words. 'We've known each other a long time and I count us friends of a sort, and I don't want to see you hurt.'

Jean found words at last. 'What on earth are ee bletheran aboot?'

Sarah drew a deeper breath, adjusted her head scarf and went on to tell how in her own house he had been exposed. 'He was as bald as a new-laid egg,' concluded Sarah, 'and I don't think a man should cover up his faults like at.'

'I knew he was bald,' said Jean. 'At wig o his sat on his heid lek a divot. Ee didna think I was taken in by at? And fit was Mr Clove doan in your hoose anyway?'

'I invited him for a cuppie o tea.'

'Ee took a fancy til him?'

'Certainly not,' said Sarah, blushing. 'But I thought you did. You were planning til run off til Spain wi him. I saw the Spanish book on the coonter.'

'Ye had no richt til interfere in my affairs,' said Jean, and she planted her forearms on the counter. 'But I twigged him fae e start. He's just a chancer and a charmer, and I was just stringan him along. Did ee think at peedie mannie had turned my heid? I havna comen doon wi e last shoor o rain. Although I dinna think it was any o your business.'

Sarah blushed again. 'Weel . . . eh . . . I suppose it wasna, but ee ken . . .'

'At's men all ower for ee,' sighed Jean. 'Ee canna trust them one little bit. Did ee give him a dinner?'

'Eh, no,' admitted Sarah, 'Just a fly cup, and he left before he even finished it. Hiding his wig inside his jacket. He got an awful fricht, poor Mr Clove. I feel sorry for him.'

Jean glared across the counter, as if this would stiffen Sarah's resolve. At that moment, the door of the shop opened and some bairns came in to buy sweeties. Jean told them to line up and behave themselves, and Sarah retired among the shelves to inspect the cat food.

*   *   *

'Fit happened til ee at ee ran away and left me? Fine partner ee turned oot til be.' Pogo's voice was filled with outrage because Dreep had abandoned him to face the likely wrath of Lady Roster alone.

'She put me under citizen's arrest but then gave me a suspended sentence,' went on Pogo. 'In fact, it worked oot all richt. We're goan til see Magnus, e two o us. Then he'll listen.'

'See Magnus aboot what?' Dreep's sister Utsira was washing dishes.

'At's a secret,' said Pogo. 'Ee coman for a pint?'

Utsira broke in again. 'No, he isna. He's got til tidy e shed. It's fill o trock at he keeps takan home fae e dump.'

'It's no trock,' protested Dreep. 'It's good stuff. I'm savan it for e next car-boot sale.'

'I wish ee would pit it back in e bins far ee got it,' said his sister.

'Ee havna got a car,' said Pogo.

'I ken but I'm savan for one, now at I've passed my test. Aye, I fancy a pint.'

'Good,' said Pogo, rising. 'I'll let ee buy me one til show at I forgive ee for runnan off on me. Come on.'

*   *   *

Cattach was looking uncommonly pleased with himself, yet at the same time had a faraway look in his eyes. 'You know this,' he murmured dreamily to Bowser, 'it's a marvellous thing til discover in your mature years at all iss time you've been a grandfaither and you never kent.'

'Ee widna have kent yet if I hadna telt ee,' growled Bowser.

'Aye, well, maybe, but it's still a marvellous thing. It's grand having a granddochter without having til go through e hassle o livan wi her grandmither or her mither all at time. Did I tell ee she sent me an email? They're safe back in Thorshaven now.'

'Ee've telt me five times.'

'Well, it's a marvellous thing.'

Bowser yawned. 'Och aye, at's e way.'

Cattach watched his friend's mouth slowly close. 'D'ye ken what yawning's for?'

'Eh?'

'I think its purpose is deep cleansing. It rids the body o toxic gases at gather in the lungs. In fact I think I'll write til the *Groat* aboot it.'

Bowser sighed. 'When was it ee said you're goan til e Faroes?'

*   *   *

Jean and Sarah sipped their tea together. Sarah could not remember the last time she had been in Jean's kitchen and it was a mark of their sudden solidarity that she was there now. It was a nice little kitchen, thought Sarah, although the curtains didn't quite match the paper and there was a stain on the wall beside the cooker that looked unhealthily mysterious. They sipped their tea and commented to each other on its taste, and the sweetness of the biscuits, in fragments though they were, as they came from a dropped packet.

'I micht have been very mad if it had been any other wumman but yoursel at had invited Mr Clove for a cup o tea,' said Jean lightly.

'Oh?' said Sarah.

'I mean,' said Jean, 'he'll be a whilie yet before he's at retiring age.'

Sarah's brows met. What was this limmer hinting at? That Mr Clove was too young for her? Oh but Jean could be two-faced. 'Age doesn't seem to matter much nowadays,' she said gaily. For example, she thought, there had been that item in the *News of the World* about a toyboy.

'What d'ye think e world looks like fae a man's point o view?' asked Jean suddenly.

'Oh mercy . . . weel . . . now at's a conundrum,' said Sarah in a voice that hinted that, even if she knew the answer, she had no intention of revealing it.

The bell above the shop door broke in on them. 'Oh, fa's at now?' cried Jean and, putting down her cup, she heaved her bulk upright and went off to the shop.

Sarah realised that she was now alone in Jean's kitchen and had already begun to think of the opportunities this offered when she heard from the direction of the shop: 'And I've come to thank you, both you and Miss Job.'

Trembling, Sarah put down her cup, wiped crumbs from her lap and followed Jean. There, just inside the shop door, his arms clutched around two bouquets of flowers, stood Mr Clove. His head was thrust forward between the roses and the most remarkable thing about it was not the cheery smile or the dancing eyes but the complete absence of hair.

'I want to thank you both,' he cried. 'All these years I was embarrassed about being bald. Not any more. I've just burnt my wigs on the links. You've set me free, both of you. I feel liberated. Baldness is beautiful!'

Will Pogo realise his dream of riches from the Holy Well of Saint Erik? Will Jean or Miss Sarah Job ever find a man? Will Magnus Stroup receive his OBE? Life in Brimster goes on.

Glossary

Readers who have the misfortune not to be familiar with the Caithness dialect may find the following notes an aid to understanding.

aboothan wi	in the vicinity of
-an	The Caithness equivalent of the -ing verbal ending in standard English. In nouns it changes to -ane
bicht	a loop in a rope, a bight
bool	a large stone, a boulder
boyagie	a small boy
chiel	a man
chuchter	a bumpkin
clep	a fisherman's gaff
dwaum	a trance
e	the, the definite article
ee	you
ere	there
evenow	just now
fa	who?
fa achts at chiel?	who is that man's father?
fae	from
fan	when?
fang	to move laboriously
fann	a snowdrift
far ben	well in with someone
far ee twa fae?	where do you two come from?
fat/fit?	what?
feint a thing	not a thing
flech	a flea

foosim	dirty
gadgie	a man
geiks	tall weeds such as nettles or cow parsley
Groat	The local name for the weekly local newspaper, the *John O'Groat Journal*
humbowg	a nuisance
-ie	universal diminutive ending
ill-naitered	bad-tempered
iss	this
kittled	tickled
lassagie	a little girl
loon	boy, young man. 'Loonie' is a diminutive
maa	seagull
newse	to converse
Ola	the colloquial name for the *Saint Ola*, for many years the ferry between Caithness and Orkney
park	a field
peat bank	the place where peats are cut from the moor
peedie	little
plucker	a shore fish that erects spines when it is angry or disturbed
revvle	a tangle
rift	to burp
scarf	a cormorant
skate gump	the head and backbone of a skate, ideal for shellfish bait
skitteran army	colloquial expression for cattle, or any group of beings that excrete copiously
slater	a woodlouse
skorrie	a young seagull
sorn	to search
spend	to separate lambs from their mothers before a sale
stab	a fencepost
Stroma	the name of the only island in Caithness. Its permanent population long since gone, it stands in the Pentland Firth

swackness	suppleness
til	to
toe-pointer	an amateurish and deplorable way by which to kick a football
wether	a castrated male lamb

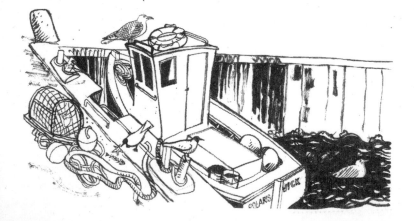